THREADS OF HOPE

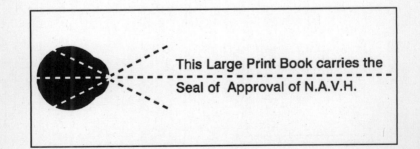

THREADS OF HOPE

CHRISTA ALLAN

THORNDIKE PRESS
A part of Gale, Cengage Learning

Detroit • New York • San Francisco • New Haven, Conn • Waterville, Maine • London

LIBRARY OF CONGRESS CATALOGING-IN-PUBLICATION DATA

Allan, Christa.
    Threads of hope / by Christa Allan. — Large print edition.
        pages ; cm. — (Thorndike Press large print clean reads) (Quilts of love series)
    ISBN 978-1-4104-6271-8 (hardcover) — ISBN 1-4104-6271-4 (hardcover) 1. Women periodical editors—Fiction. 2. AIDS (Disease) and the arts. 3. Quilting—Fiction. 4. Large type books. I. Title.
PS3601.L4125T48 2013b
813'.6—dc23   2013032230

Published in 2013 by arrangement with Abingdon Press

Printed in the United States of America
1 2 3 4 5 6 7 17 16 15 14 13

To the families and friends of the men, women, and children whose lives will be forever stitched together on The AIDS Memorial Quilt. Remember. Understand. Share the lessons. Act.

ACKNOWLEDGMENTS

Much like the varied and various panels stitched together to compose a quilt that is unique and a reflection of all those who participated in its completion, so too is this novel. Because of the contributions of others, each offering a special talent or wisdom, this novel is in your hands.

Thanks to Abingdon Press for their continued support: to Senior Acquisitions Editor — Fiction Ramona Richards and Teri Wilhelms, who edited the novel, and to everyone there whose dedication makes publishing possible.

I deeply appreciate my agent Sandra Bishop, who tirelessly stitches me together every time I unravel. I probably should enroll her in Thimble-of-the-Month Club (not that there is one, but if there was, she'd be a charter member).

Jenny B. Jones . . . how can I thank you except to give you a few weeks of peace between novels. I've leaned on you (okay, maybe sometimes poured concrete and used you as a foundation) through texts, telephone, tweets, e-mails, and gchats. I've exhausted every means and method of communication in seeking your help, and you still haven't (yet) moved to an unknown location on some unknown planet.

Thanks to Shelley, whose plotting skills save me, and to Carole and Carrie for calling me to make sure I've not impaled myself on a red pen. Thanks to the lunch bunch for laughter: Michelle, Meredith, Tammie, Jennifer, Kim, Tracey, Adam, and Andrew.

Without my brother John and my brother-in-law Ricky, every meal would be Coke Zero, popcorn, and chocolate. It's incredibly reassuring to know that, every day, I'm only twenty-three steps away from encouragement, food, and love.

My children, Michael, Erin (and Andrae), Shannon, Sarah, and John (all now old enough to be adult-ren), continue to claim me as their mother even when I'm at my craziest. And, of course, my forever love and gratitude to my husband Ken, who has learned the art of self-preservation during my writing and of us-preservation when I'm not.

8

Thank you God for making all of the above possible.

1

After three years, it finally happened.

Janie Bettencourt announced her promotion. She would be moving from Houston to New York to become Senior Editor of *Trends* magazine.

The promotion Nina O'Malley had hoped would be her own.

And, as if that news wasn't enough to justify Nina adding banana splits as main dish items on her diet, ice cream became its own food group after Janie added that joining her would be staff photographer Brady Lambert.

The Brady who, years ago, promised her the moon. The Brady who, later, spun out of her orbit and splashed down in Janie's. The Brady Lambert whom Nina had hoped would be her own.

When was she going to learn to wait for the other shoe to drop before assuming she could celebrate?

Earlier that morning, when she'd spotted an email message from Elise Johnson, the Executive Editor, Nina allowed herself the luxury of dreaming. Elise's personal emails were infrequent, at least in her in-box, and generally, no frills, as if she'd be charged by the word count. So, she wasn't at all offended when she read the brief request: "My office. Nine o'clock. Important matter to discuss. EJ." In fact, she was elated. And she remained so for the next fifty-four minutes, not counting her elevator time to the seventh floor where she was ushered into Elise's office.

In less time than it took for Nina to arrive in the starkly modern office of the executive editor, disappointment introduced itself. Later, when the elevator door swished open to reveal Janie, Nina felt like a contestant on a game show who'd guessed wrongly and seen what she might have won.

The weight of Elise's remarks might have pushed Nina to the second floor almost as efficiently as the elevator: *Structurally correct writing, but lacked style and passion. More initiative and less predictability. Network. Move out of your comfort zone.* Elise challenged Nina to convince her that she'd be making a mistake not to promote her. "We're considering other markets like

Atlanta and Nashville, perhaps Los Angeles. One of those could be yours. Show me what you can do."

By the time Janie gathered the staff and squealed her news, Nina had power walked to Starbucks and returned caffeinated and composed. She smiled in Janie's direction, grateful Janie couldn't read her thoughts to know her angelic face came from imagining a subway door closing on one of her size 6 Ferragamo shoes.

Just as the image was becoming crystal clear in Nina's mind, a tidal wave of a voice in her head crashed over that picture and left behind the sound of her mother's words: *"You're being so petty, my dear. God doesn't like ugly, you know."* Nina mentally shushed her mother who, even more than twenty miles away, could still inject an admonition into her daughter's nerve center of guilt.

Sheila Hudson O'Malley married Nina's father Patrick not long after they graduated from high school and then stayed home to mother two children into semi-adulthood. What would she know about fickle boyfriends and dashed career dreams? "Sure, mother. Easy for you to say," Nina muttered as she diverted her attention from the fawning frenzy over Janie to rearrange the clutter on her desk. She hoped to unearth her iPad from underneath what looked like an office supply store explosion of paper that had landed there.

"Were you talking to me?"

Nina paused between lifting legal pads to turn toward her cubicle-mate, Daisy Jeffers, who had scooted her desk chair past her partition, and now stared at her. As usual, her dark hair sprouted from the top of her head like sprinkler arms. She was always one strong wind short of being propelled above ground level.

"No. I was talking to my mother." Nina resumed her excavation.

"Well, I'm assuming the one in your head since I don't smell Chanel No. 5 in the vicinity. And, anyway . . ." she bit into her apple.

Now that Nina found her iPad lurking in her desk drawer under a stack of folders and three expired restaurant coupons, she focused on Daisy. "Are you aware how absolutely annoying that is?"

Daisy swallowed. "You mean her?" Still holding her half-eaten apple, Daisy bent her arm over her head and motioned in the general direction of the newly promoted.

Nina flipped open the leather cover to find her interview notes. "Not Janie. You. Can you wait until before or after your thoughts, not between them, to eat? It's so maddening waiting for you to finish chewing . . ." She paused.

Her mother's voice. She heard her mother's voice, the one that forever seemed marinated in exasperation, spill out of her own mouth. She looked up at Daisy. "You just got a whiff of Chanel No. 5 didn't you?" Nina gave way to the defeat and disappointment and flopped into her chair.

Daisy pinched her nose for a moment and grimaced. "A serious overdose." Not an unexpected reply from someone who smelled as if she'd spritzed herself with bottled spring rain, newly mown summer grass, and a hint of an autumn bonfire. She tossed her apple core into her stainless steel eco-lunchbox, wiped her hands with her cotton napkin, and rolled herself closer to Nina. Almost ten years younger than Nina, Daisy exuded a wisdom beyond her age. As a child, she slept in a car for weeks until her single mother found a homeless shelter for them. Daisy figured living on the streets was poverty's answer to accelerated learning. Nina suspected Daisy's minimalist approach to the externals in her life — clothing, furniture, car — balanced the burden of her emotional life.

"It's just not your time," said Daisy. "There will be a season for you, too."

Nina felt as if she'd just been patted on the head and told to run along and play. "I'd like to wallow in my pity party a bit longer before you start breaking it up with your New Age-y philosophies," she responded.

Daisy smiled. A reaction Nina found more annoying than the smattering of applause earlier that followed Janie's news.

"Well, I wouldn't be a worthy friend if I didn't at least try to save you from yourself. And, anyway, how much of a party is it if you're the only one with an invitation?"

"Speaking of invitations . . ."

Nina was as startled to see Janie materialize as Daisy appeared to be when she heard her voice. Daisy slowly swiveled her chair and looked up at the leggy blonde who leaned against the gray dividing wall separating their desks from the receptionist's. "Whoa. How did you do that? Is magically transporting yourself part of the new job description?"

Janie tilted her head, placed her forefinger on her cheek, and became a perfect model for "deep in thought." Except for the smirk. She dropped the pose and looked at Nina. "I suppose having my finger on the pulse of

16

the magazine is a requisite for effective management. Wouldn't you agree?"

Daisy and Nina exchanged eye contact then stared at Janie.

"So . . . anyway . . . back to invitations." Janie reached into the pocket of her flouncy skirt and silenced the pinging on her cell phone. "I'm having a cozy going-away dinner at my condo in two weeks. Of course, you're both invited. Bra and I are hosting it together."

"Bra," which she pronounced like "hey" was her special name for Brady, used only when not in his presence. The first time Janie uttered it in the office, it sliced through any thread of expectation Nina held for a future with him. She suspected the affectation was Janie's unseen electric collar around Brady, but instead of confining him, it zapped a warning to any women on the prowl contemplating new territory. Or one like Nina, who hoped for an open gate.

Over time, most of the staff became adept at avoiding eye-rolls when Janie blathered on about Bra. Though Daisy refused to abandon the idea that she might one day write a story about Bra and Janie's relationship. She hoped Victoria's Secret would think it a grand tale of a woman who referred to her lingerie in third person.

Now, faced with the prospect of swallowing food while enduring Brady and Janie, Nina rifled through her mental file of excuses. She barely had time to consider the choices when Daisy said, "We wouldn't dream of missing an opportunity to send you off on your new adventure." She glanced at Nina. "Would we?"

What Nina wanted to do at that moment was send Daisy twirling back across the partition. Instead, she mumbled something about making sure she'd be free, grabbed her iPad, and hoped when she swiped her calendar she'd find an event so monumental it would be impossible to attend the dinner. But no. No White House interview, no late night talk show appearance, and no undercover expose planned. Just a reminder to drop off her clothes at the cleaner and buy a case of dog food. *Pathetic. My life needs a makeover.* She stared at the socially vacant month of April. "Well, I do have two things I'm committed to that day . . ." Nina avoided looking at Daisy and told Janie she didn't see any reason why she shouldn't be able to finish in time to attend the dinner.

Janie clapped her hands. "Wonderful! Check your emails because I'm sending e-vites with all the information and directions —" A piano riff sounded from her pocket. She pulled out her cell phone, then excused herself with an, "I have to answer this one." The rhythm of her stiletto heels click-clacking on the wood floors accompanied her departure.

"Commitments? Since when did you have commitments?" Daisy could have replaced "commitments" with "children" and sounded no less surprised.

It was, after all, a word Nina had iced, figuratively speaking, along with others like *engagement, marriage, wedding gown,* and *honeymoon.* If only Nina could remember to forget some commitments in her life as much as she forgot to remember others, she wouldn't have to place her dreams in the freezer.

"I consider feeding Manny and wearing clean clothes important responsibilities. Especially since they both cost more than I ever anticipated." She had adopted her hybrid dog with the dachshund body and poodle hair from the local animal shelter almost a year ago. When she brought him home, she named him Manhattan and thought it clever and optimistic. Today, it just seemed ridiculous. The little runt developed severe food allergies and now required a special diet. She didn't expect him to be so high maintenance. Expectations did not seem to be working in her favor lately.

"If that works for you, then stay with it," said Daisy as she scooted her chair back to her desk. She closed her laptop, gathered her environmentally-safe assortment of bags, and wiggled her metro-nylon backpack out of the bottom drawer. "I have two more people to interview for the yoga feature, so I'll let you get back to that one-woman pity party I interrupted."

"Thanks." Nina clapped, Janie-like. "It saves me from sending an e-vite."

"You actually smiled. One small step —"

Nina grabbed a sheet of paper out of her printer and waved it in front of her. "I surrender. I surrender. No more words of wisdom."

Daisy laughed. "Okay, but the terms of surrender include walking to the stairs with me. You've been sitting so long I'm surprised you're not numb. But, the bonus is you'll make sure I actually leave. And leave you alone."

"That, my dear, is motivation enough," said Nina. She waited until the glass doors of the office shut behind them before she asked Daisy if she noted Brady's conspicuous absence from the Janie show.

"Probably not as much as you did."

Daisy's eyes swept over Nina's face, and Nina knew desperation hovered there. "You need to let go of him in both places," Daisy said as she pressed her hand first to her forehead and then to her heart. "Remember, 'There's a season for everything.' "

Nina sighed. "Is that some mantra you chant?"

Daisy pushed open the door to the stairwell. "No, but that's not a bad idea." She paused, shifted her backpack, and said, "By the way, it's not new age-y talk. It's old age-y. Very old, as in Old Testament. King Solomon."

"So, you're telling me I'm in a very long line of people who know what it's like not to get what they want? I suppose that's some comfort," said Nina drily. Comfort and God hadn't been synonymous for her since before her brother was hospitalized. It wasn't so much that she gave up on God. She just chose not to give in to Him.

"The real comfort is, the line didn't end there," said Daisy. "See you tomorrow. Take care of yourself."

Nina watched Daisy and couldn't help but notice that, despite the baggage she carried, Daisy floated down the stairs as if she carried no weight at all.

2

"Do you know the origin of the word *dead-line*?"

"Hmm. Let me think. Does it have something to do with cutting off service to the cell phone of your friend who persists in calling you when she knows you're working?" Nina's eyes stayed focused on the screen while her fingers continued their waltz over the keys of her laptop. The few paragraphs she needed to finish the piece tapped their feet in the waiting room of her brain. If she didn't concentrate, they'd fly out the door and, from experience, she knew coercing them to return was almost impossible.

"You have me on speaker phone, don't you?" Aretha's accusation was as loud as it was unmistakable. "That's it. I'm buying you a Bluetooth device for those perky ears of yours."

Nina bit her bottom lip, typed in a few

key words to pacify the paragraphs, and picked up her cell phone. "You're off now," she mashed the speaker button, then held the phone to her ear as she plowed through the contents of her purse hoping to excavate a buried Snickers bar. "And I have no idea where deadline originated, and I don't need to know at this moment because I'm less than an hour away from meeting mine." She pulled out an empty Twix wrapper, two smashed cheese crackers, and an aging peppermint. Her stomach rumbled in disappointment. "What's up? And the microwave version." They'd been roommates a little over a year, and Nina learned Aretha couldn't tell someone the time without detailing where, when, and why she bought her watch.

"Well, if you'd bother to listen to your voicemails you'd know what's up. The fact that you're so cranky ought to remind you we're waiting for you at Carrabba's. It was your idea to eat Italian this month. Remember?"

Girls' Night Out. She forgot. Again. "It can't be seven o'clock already . . . ." Had it been that long since Daisy left? She stood and looked around the room. With the exception of a few interns huddled around *Grey's Anatomy,* she was the lone staff writer left in the office.

Squinting to check the clock in the corner of her computer screen, she heard Aretha's voice, "No. It's almost thirty minutes later."

Nina figured by the time she finished checking and rechecking the article before sending it off to Elise, the girls would already be ordering or eating dessert. Doubtful they'd want to wait for her to catch up. Not that she could blame them. And if she wasn't already holding her breath to button her jeans, she'd go straight for the tiramisu and skip dinner altogether. With enough misery threaded into her voice to gather a bit of sympathy, Nina said, "I'm so sorry. I have to get this story in on time. Especially after today . . . but I'll tell you more about that later. Please ask the girls to forgive me for making them wait."

She truly meant the part about being sorry. In college, Nina chose not to rush for a sorority, mainly because she never received an invitation. It wasn't until she and Aretha became roommates that she began to let loose of the notion that all women her age were younger versions of her mother, eager to provide a list of her shortcomings in the name of helping her become the way God meant her to be. Nina felt comfortable with this group, and she didn't want to jeopardize that friendship by being the lone no-show every month.

"You're just lucky we all like you or else we'd have voted you off the dinner table by now," said Aretha. "I suppose you want an order to go."

Nina thought she felt her stomach applaud. "Yes, please. Pasta Weesie."

"You know you order that every time? I think you just like saying the name," she said and sounded less frustrated and more amused. "Let me hang up or else they'll start thinking I'm redecorating the kitchen or something."

Aretha, in her last semester of interior design school, had a "fabulous idea to make this room pop" almost everywhere they went. At the last dinner, the group threatened to blindfold her just to have a conversation not focused on window treatments or paint colors.

Knowing she'd be met by fettuccine Alfredo with shrimp motivated Nina to push herself through the article, assembling what remained like puzzle pieces, snapping them into place until the picture was complete. Not that profiling candidates for local county elections made for riveting writing. And that was exactly the problem. Nina hoped there was a story waiting for her to find it. A story that would prompt Elise to maybe send a two-line email. A story that would begin to pave her way to the Big Apple.

"Miss O'Malley?"

Startled, Nina's body hiccupped. She took a deep breath and recognized the lilac perfume Shannon, one of the interns, typically wore. Nina turned to face her. "Now that I know it's you, what scares me more is your using 'Miss.' It ages me five years."

"I'm sorry." A smile flickered across Shannon's face as she slid her pearl drop back and forth on her necklace chain. "We're all leaving. Do you want us, me, to wait for you?" The other interns, three young women who looked like they shopped in each other's closets, hovered a cubicle away.

Nina stretched back in her chair, mowed her fingers through her entirely-too-short hair, then stared at her monitor. "Not much more to go." She looked at Shannon and realized she didn't even know her last name. Or even what she did for the magazine. *Have I been that cocooned in my own life?* Earlier, Elise encouraged her to network. Nina realized at that moment she better begin in her own office. But clearly not now.

"So . . . um . . . does that mean it's okay for us to go?" Shannon asked as if she had

dropped Nina off for her first day of kinder-
garten and needed the teacher's permission
to leave.

Distracted by her own shortcomings,
she'd created another by not answering
Shannon's question. "Oh, of course, of
course," she replied and sounded perkier
than she meant to. "I shouldn't be long,
and Nelson can walk me to my car."

"Well, I'll see you tomorrow," said Shannon, and she trailed after her friends as they
headed out the door.

It didn't register until after Nina had
clicked "send" that she forgot to thank
Shannon for thinking about her. How incon-
siderate.

Nina didn't know if she heard her mother's voice just then or her own.

Did her mother always have to be right?

Nina had asked herself that question, she
supposed, since she could first express a
coherent thought. The answer didn't
change. Sometimes Sheila wasn't 100 percent right, but on some weird pie chart of
probabilities, there would always be a slice
for her mother. Little wonder her father
spent so much time shrugging his shoulders
and shuffling into his mancave when his

wife's pronouncements fell like stinging rain.

In sixth grade, Nina became friends with Elizabeth Hamilton, and Sheila told her she should stay away from her because "that girl's nothing but trouble." With every trouble-free year that passed, Nina reminded her mother what she had said about her friend. Four years of trouble-free, until the tenth grade when Elizabeth had a "stomach virus" that eight months later was named Andy. And Sheila reminded her daughter what she had said about her friend.

During her junior year of high school, Nina started being invited to parties given by girls who wore shoes that cost more than all of her clothes. They didn't seem to mind picking her up in their sleek cars, the ones that didn't have names, just initials. They even let her wear their dresses to school dances where the beautiful girls met the handsome boys, and they moved inside their own force field that kept everyone else away. One day, on the way to the women's Bible study at church, her mother said, "Those girls are just buttering you up to use you. One day, they're going to drop you like a hot potato."

Nina laughed. "What could I possibly have that those girls would ever want? Is it too hard for you to believe popular kids could like me?"

Some days after school, Nina would be invited to one of their houses, the ones kept behind gates. They'd ask their maids to fix them something to eat, escape to the kids' den where they would listen to music, watch television, and complain about homework. They were so very impressed with Nina's ability to understand calculus, analyze poetry, and write essays. They asked for her help, flattered her. It felt good to be needed. She noticed, though, as weeks passed, that the more she did to help them, the less they did to help themselves. When Nina refused to write Courtney's research paper because she could barely complete her own, she faded from their sight a little bit every day. Until one day, she was completely invisible. And Sheila reminded her daughter of what she had said about her friends.

Her first relationship in college ended when, after almost a year of dating, Adam informed her he wasn't "ready to commit to anything more serious." Sheila said "he was up to no good." Three months later, he married her roommate.

Nina spent her life walking through the mine field of her mother's judgments, and no matter where she stepped, something

29

was going to blow up. Tonight, forgetting to thank the intern? Not even a minor blast.

Nina shut down her laptop, slipped her feet back into her not-at-all sensible suede peep-toe shoes, and decided fettuccine and an upcoming story on the new ambulance service weren't compatible. All she needed for home was herself. She hoisted her purse onto her shoulder and headed for the door when she remembered she forgot to email Daisy about a possible interview with one of the preservationist candidates she profiled. Since she was only a few steps away from Daisy's desk, Nina pulled a blank sheet of paper out of the printer, jotted the information, and set it on her calendar pad next to a screaming yellow sticky note. Certainly, Daisy couldn't miss that. Neither could Nina because what Daisy had written on it shocked her: "Ask JB about the opening in NY."

3

As soon as she put her key into the lock, Nina heard Manny's canine symphony of yelps, barks, and squeals on the other side of the door. She scooped him up after she walked in because, if she didn't, he'd be doing figure eights around her legs until she did. "Okay, okay, little man, I'm happy to see you, too," she said as she petted Manny and calmed his enthusiastic, cold-nose nuzzling greeting.

Aretha stood at the kitchen sink filling a teakettle with water. She looked over her shoulder at Nina and smiled. "You know, I hope to find a husband who's as excited to see me come home as that dog is to see you."

Nina laughed and released the wiggling puppy who headed to his water bowl, his stubby legs causing him to toddle on the oak floors like a canine Charlie Chaplin. "I'd be willing to sacrifice some of the excitement if he didn't have doggy breath." She hung her purse on the hall tree and felt her body sigh in relief as if it had just been permitted to acknowledge it was tired. Nina pulled off her shoes and left them at the foot of the stairs before sitting on one of the kitchen barstools. "I'm so glad we ended up living here in the city; otherwise, I might have had to spend the night at the office."

"You're so welcome," Aretha told Nina and smiled, knowing they shared the memory of that decision. Nina, with the exception of college dorms, grew up in neighborhoods where the ranch style homes differed only by their brick color and front door placement. After college, she moved into an apartment complex that wasn't much different. Coming home at night required close attention to make certain the door you attempted to unlock was your own. But, it was close to her job then and, even after she was hired by *Trends,* she grew accustomed to the long drive.

Her choice of rentals was one of the few intersections of belief that Aretha and Brady, the then Brady, had. When he asked if she planned to move closer when the lease expired, Nina had shrugged and said, "I'm not sure. It's not that bad."

The two of them had driven to Baldwin

Park to let Manny, just months old then, experience grass and sunshine and other wonders of nature he couldn't see from his kennel in Nina's kitchen. Brady had stopped the game of fetch he played with the puppy to look at Nina. "Don't you want more from life than, 'it's not bad'?" She sensed, by the way he averted his eyes so quickly, that he could see she'd never given it a thought.

Aretha had been dating Franklin, a friend of Brady's, when they met. The four of them would often meet for dinner or brunch on Sunday mornings. At first glance, the two women seemed the unlikeliest of friends. Nina was as fair as Aretha was dark, as tall as she was short. While Aretha kept her wits about her, Nina scattered hers everywhere. They became fast friends, the kind of comfortable that allowed them to be quiet or rowdy in one another's presence, and knowing which one the other most needed. Their relationships with the men in their lives ended, one sputtering to a close, the other screeched over the finish line. Instead of feeling abandoned, the two young women picked themselves up, dusted themselves off, and started all over again.

When they'd first committed to become roomies, Nina had thought she and Aretha should consider renting a garden home in one of the upstart suburban communities miles outside of Houston. Manny would have a yard, and they wouldn't have to worry about crime. Aretha countered that since Manny was smaller than a five-pound bag of sugar and would spend almost all of his time inside, a yard the size of a beach towel would be sufficient. "And you will have to deal with crime," she'd told Nina, "because if I have to drive back and forth to school and work fighting that traffic, I'll want to kill you myself. Plus, a woman with cornrows named Aretha has no business being anywhere but the city."

But now her cornrows were long, loose braids whose movements reflected an energized or subdued Aretha at any given time. She placed a bag of Earl Grey tea in one of the vintage cups from her collection, this one decorated with delicate violets and sprigs of greenery. "Guess my evening ritual will include nuking that dinner of yours," Aretha said and took a lemon for her tea and a to-go box out of the refrigerator.

Nina ran her bare feet along the bottom rung of the chair trying to restore her cramped toes to life. "I had one of those horrible, no good, terrible, awful days. I felt like Alexander in that children's book. And it started this morning." Elbows on the counter, cradling her face in her hands, Nina might have fallen asleep except for the lush smell of garlic and butter and rosemary escaping from the microwave. And Manny barking at his empty food bowl.

"Mister, I fed you earlier. Don't pretend you've been neglected just because your momma's home." Aretha always translated his barks, growls, whines, head tilts, and chirps into words, and he almost always ignored hers. He circled the bowl as if to reassure himself he'd not missed a nibble, eyed Aretha, then Nina, and settled himself in his dog bed. "He's pouting," Aretha concluded. "He'll get over it."

Knowing Aretha took this conversation seriously, Nina just nodded her head and tried not to smile. Especially since, after hearing Aretha's voice, Manny turned his head away from them and faced the wall.

She transferred Nina's dinner to a plate, "Take this, you can tell me your sad story while I do my homework." She nodded in the direction of the den where a mini-library spilled over the sofa cushions.

Nina sat in the worn leather chair next to the sofa. She draped a placemat across her lap and balanced her plate as she propped her feet on the glass-topped coffee table. Between bites, she narrated her dreadful day, ending with the cryptic note on Daisy's desk.

"Give her the benefit of the doubt. Maybe all those initials are wildly incidental," Aretha said in that voice she used when she complimented someone's rather ordinary-looking baby. She didn't sound convincing then either. Her legs tucked under as she sat on the sofa, Aretha had formed a moat of books and magazines around herself in search of historical photographs for her upcoming design assignment.

"You couldn't even make eye contact with me when you said that. If you don't believe it, why do you want me to?" Nina ate the shrimp she'd stabbed with her fork and waited for Aretha's response.

"Look at this stunning Louis XIV armoire," said Aretha, her brown eyes lit with a reverent awe as she held up a picture of a massive wardrobe with a star of Bethlehem carved on each door. "Sorry." She closed the magazine. "Got distracted." She rearranged an almost toppling stack of art books, unwound her legs and stretched them out on the ottoman. "I doubt if there's an inner office conspiracy at *Trends*. Just ask Daisy tomorrow."

Nina looked up from her pasta-twirling. "Sure. I'll ask her what the note on her desk, not mine, meant. She wouldn't at all think it might be an invasion of her privacy. And, anyway, she's not once expressed an interest in going to New York. Wouldn't she have said something when I told her months ago that I wanted that position? Do you think . . ." She stopped, her voice shifted into worrisome. "Do you think maybe she wanted to go? But not with me?"

"If you were any more neurotic, I would have to take you to work and pray someone would take pity on me and commit you. Those county mental health specialists don't fool around," said Aretha, her words edged with just enough seriousness to pinch Nina's ego. "Maybe it's time for you to re-assess." She looked over Nina's shoulder. "And take Manny for a walk."

Nina looked down to see her dog, holding one end of his leash between his teeth, the rest of it snaked behind him.

"See, even he knows, sometimes you just have to be upfront about what you want," said Aretha.

4

Nina pulled away from the drive-through at Starbucks when her mother's phone number flashed on her navigation screen. Did Sheila O'Malley feel a shift in her frugal universe because her daughter just bought a latte for the price of a pound of coffee? Nina decided to stay on the feeder road and not attempt merging into the early morning Houston freeway. Verbally sparring with her mother while negotiating the traffic version of dodge ball — could it get any worse? *Probably not. Get the worst over with now, and the rest of the day will seem like the set of a Disney movie.* She had the cloud waiting for her to answer; the silver lining couldn't be far behind.

She took a deep breath, pressed the call button, and prepared herself for battle. "Good morning, Mother."

"Are you in your car?" It sounded like an accusation, not a question.

"I'm on my way to the office," said Nina and wished she could close her eyes during their conversation. For some reason, shutting out the world in the soft blackness inside herself made her feel less anxious during these painful volleys. "Is there something you need?" She used her best chirpy voice even after she pushed her brake hard to avoid smashing the car in front of her. Her purse toppled onto the floorboard and burped out its contents.

"Need? Do I need something? Why would I need something to call my daughter? I just wanted to remind you about Sunday dinner," she said. "That's all. You know how much it means to your father to have you there."

"So, what are you saying? That my being there isn't important to you? And how could I forget about a dinner you call every week to remind me about that's been a standing appointment so long my car would drive there without me?"

But, of course, Nina asked none of those questions. She simply said, "I'll be there."

Nina took the stairs instead of the elevator, a sort of aerobic decompression to move the tightness in her chest down her body and out through her feet, leaving the tension behind with each pounding step. *Why do I let her get under my skin like a splinter?*

She knew the reason. She'd known for decades. She was her parents' only child. Their only surviving child. When Nina was nine, her older brother Thomas came home after his second year at the University of Miami. At first, her parents told their friends Thomas wasn't sure he wanted to return, that he might want to attend college closer to home. Nina remembered running to hug her brother, excited about the possibility of his being close. But when the summer ended, he didn't enroll at a Texas university or any other one. Thomas started helping his friend Rick, a housepainter, which annoyed and disappointed their mother who accused him of wasting his intelligence, his potential to make something out of his life. He told her, "It's what I put in to life that matters. Every day I get to make something fresh and new. That is enough for me, for now."

That was the only part of their conversation Nina heard that day when she walked in to the kitchen after the yellow school bus lurched away from their street. Thomas looked tired, which, as she headed to her room as per her mother's orders, she understood on some level even then. The emotional tug-of-war with their mother required endurance training. Sheila continued to tug, but eventually Thomas let go of the rope. Nothing to fight for when there was no one to fight with.

Less than a year later, Sheila picked Nina up from school, an act in itself a signal that something was awry in the O'Malley home, to tell her that Thomas was gone. At first, Nina thought she meant he'd left the hospital where he'd been, but her mother told her that he wasn't coming home. Ever. After Thomas's funeral, her father retreated into his wordless shrugs, and her mother donned the armor of the self-righteous because, as she told anyone with an ear, "I told him that he wasn't meant to waste his potential that way."

Twenty years later, Nina still couldn't penetrate the shield of her mother's emotional defenses. And, like her brother, the pain of trying became much greater than the fear of not. But now she needed to sharpen her own sword, fight her own battles. And two of those battles sat in offices on the other side of the *Trends* door that she now opened.

She stepped into the lobby, and the aroma of hazelnut coffee greeted her before Michelle, the new receptionist, had a chance to. She started a month ago, replacing a twenty-something who wore clothes on the verge of vintage and kept an iPod bud in one ear and the receptionist's headset in the other. The day Elise overheard her tell a client to hold on, "my song's almost over," she fired her. Two days later she interviewed Michelle, who looked like she could have been Elise's older sister though she was probably old enough to be Elise's mother. The perfect combination of maturity and chic. Michelle was on the phone, but she mouthed "hello" to Nina when she passed and pointed to a tray of scones and muffins on the hospitality table next to the coffee. Nina stopped to fix herself a cup of coffee and carried it and a cinnamon scone to her desk, whispering "Thanks," to Michelle on her way.

Nina hadn't yet decided how to approach Daisy about the cryptic note, so walking down the hall to the offices, she felt a pinprick of anxiety. *Ridiculous. Daisy is a friend, not your mother. She's not out to sabotage you. This could be your silver lining after the storm.* She took a breath and summoned a smile.

But Daisy wasn't sitting in her chair eating her predictable breakfast of yogurt, blueberries, and walnuts; in fact, the desk looked just as it did the night before when Nina left. After setting her coffee and scone down, Nina walked around the gray partitioned wall and asked Carole, in charge of ad sales, if she'd seen Daisy or heard if she was out on assignment somewhere. Neither Carole nor her sales reps knew anything. She was about to call Michelle, when her phone buzzed. It was Michelle telling her that Daisy had left a voicemail that she wouldn't be in the office for a few days. "She said she had unexpected family business to take care of, but she'd be back on Monday."

"Did she mention where she was going?" Not that her destination was any of Nina's business, but Daisy wasn't known for doing disappearing-from-the-office acts. Most of the time, convincing her to disappear from the office was the problem.

"Hmm. No. No, she didn't. But you have her cell number, right? Maybe you could call and find out, see if she needs us to do anything."

After Michelle hung up, Nina made it through half her scone and still the "family business" angle confused her. Daisy never mentioned her father in any of their conversations, and all she ever said about her mother was that they had made peace with each other. She knew she didn't have any siblings because they'd had the "only child" discussion soon after they met. And why didn't Daisy call her? They didn't spend too much time together outside of the magazine, but they did text and phone chat at least about office business. So, if Daisy wanted to contact her, she could. Nina checked for a text message, a voicemail. Nothing. She opened her laptop to check her email. Nothing from Daisy, but what she did see there could be a silver lining or another cloud in waiting.

Elise had sent her another email. "Please see me as soon as you arrive this morning."

5

Nina stared at the email from Elise, then started to roll her chair back to tell Daisy. Only there was no Daisy. No Daisy to demand that she not focus on her unmanicured hands, go-to faux-wrap dress and overdue highlights. No Daisy to reassure her that every communication from Elise was not an invitation to disaster.

She closed her email, checked her makeup using the mirror she kept in her top desk drawer, and wished praying did not seem like a foreign language. Too late to wish an Elise-summons didn't go directly to her inner child — the one biting her nails as she sat by the telephone and listened as it didn't ring.

The office stirred around her, awakened from its overnight sleep by phones that rang like alarms, doors that yawned open, and desks that claimed their owners. Still, she hadn't heard Janie's voice, so if she just pushed herself into action now, she wouldn't have to endure the knowing glances as the elevator doors closed.

Nina walked up and found Shannon, the intern from the night before, at the elevator. She held two venti-sized Starbucks' cups and wore a discombobulated expression. When she spotted Nina, she smiled as if she'd been rescued from a bad blind date.

"Are you going up, too?" Shannon rolled her eyes. "Well, that was a stupid question. Why else would you be standing at the elevator. Right?" She looked at the cups in her hands. "Guess I should've bought a caffeine jolt for myself. But I couldn't figure out how to juggle all that."

"Can I help you with one of those?" Nina stepped in the elevator first and pushed the button to keep the doors open.

"Thanks. But if you could just press seven for me, I can handle these."

"Is one of those a skinny soy chai tea latte no foam?"

"Actually, they both are," Shannon answered.

"So, you're on your way to Elise's office," said Nina, ashamedly relieved that at least she wasn't the person asked to make the coffee run before the visit.

"Right again." She held up one cup.

46

"Elise." The she hoisted the other. "Whoever orders for Elise. How did you know?"

"She's the only thing the 7th floor and chai tea have in common," Nina said as the elevator doors opened. She nodded in Shannon's direction. "Go ahead. I'm getting off here, too." And she hoped not for the last time. "Wait. I can deliver those for you."

Shannon hesitated, and Nina imagined she weighed the awkwardness of being the coffee waitress against the possible payoff of being willing to serve. Not that she blamed her. "You know, maybe it's better for you to bring them. I should stop by the bathroom first."

"Oh, okay. Then I'll see you downstairs." Shannon headed to Elise's office, while Nina veered in the direction of the bathroom that she didn't really need, but spared the intern from having to make a decision.

"Shannon said you were on your way," said Tammie, Elise's assistant. "She's expecting you."

"Thanks," Nina said and smiled when she saw the Starbucks cup by Tammie's keyboard. She wondered what came first, the order or the boss?

Nina opened the door and heard Elise's

47

voice as she entered, but she wasn't at her desk.

"Behind you," said Elise.

Nina looked back to her right and saw Elise standing over a table in a small room off her office. She'd never noticed it before, but then she had never been in Elise's office long enough to know where the doors led. Laid out on the long table were flat-plans of each page of the next issue.

"I could do this digitally, but there's something about being able to see it, large, this way that appeals to me so much more," said Elise, who continued to look at the pages in front of her. She was one of the few women Nina knew who could pull off a red pleated skirt and silk cream T-shirt without looking as if she was returning to high school. The gunmetal gray suede pumps probably helped. The metal toe seemed perfectly suited for Elise.

Nina didn't know if a response was expected, since Elise hadn't even made eye contact yet. She knew what Elise meant because sometimes, especially when she felt stuck, Nina outlined and wrote drafts of her stories on her yellow legal pads. Moving a pen across something tangible connected her to whatever she was working on at the time. But before she could move the words

48

from her brain to her lips, Elise picked her coffee cup off the table, finally looked at Nina, and said, "Let's go to my desk."

"Sure," Nina replied. *Oh, brilliant, Nina. What a sharp response.* But whatever Elise's reason for this particular summons, Nina felt confident it wasn't another cloud. Elise seemed too relaxed. When it came to terminations or demotions, Elise was a guillotine. Fast, sharp, and irreversible.

She reached in her desk drawer and handed Nina an envelope. "Here are two tickets to the We Care benefit next Friday."

The swish of panic zipped through Nina's chest because her lack of an immediate response stood between them. Nina knew that Elise knew that she didn't know enough about the benefit to reply. She watched the realization move over her face as if a window blind had been lowered to block the light.

"The We Care benefit? The fund-raiser for The AIDS Memorial Quilt?" Elise filled the quiet with a question meant to shovel enough mud out of Nina's brain to unearth the answer.

The shovel hit paydirt. "The quilt in Washington, D.C., right?" Nina unwound her fingers from the chair arm. She'd been holding on like she was preparing for an airport landing.

49

"Yes, that one. Local support groups donate quilts for a silent auction as a fundraiser. The money goes to support local projects and the NAMES Project Foundation that preserves and cares for The AIDS Memorial Quilt."

She took the envelope from Elise and wouldn't have been surprised if she snatched it right back. Now that she'd saved her head from being chopped off, Nina wondered why she was covering an event so meant for Daisy. Feature writing was definitely not her forte, and schmoozing with Houston's gilded made her uncomfortable. Daisy could handle being out of her element, especially if it involved such an important cause.

"I know you're working on the story about that local politician and questionable contracts, so you're going to have to add this one to your list. Janie will be in New York looking for an apartment. If Daisy's out longer than we or she expects, well, I don't want to take that chance." She took a sip of coffee, then looked at the cup as if someone had just handed her the wrong baby in delivery. "What is this?" Elise set the cup aside. "How difficult is it to order coffee?"

Nina assumed that was a rhetorical question, but rather than risk a conversation about Shannon being the orderer of the coffee, she asked about Daisy. "Michelle told me this morning that Daisy wouldn't be in for a while. Do you know how she's doing?" Nina tread cautiously, unsure how Elise would react to being asked information about another employee.

Elise stopped tapping her pen on her desk. "Daisy, from what I could tell by her message, is fine." She resumed the pen's previous beat, but Nina was grateful she drummed her desk pad this time. "She wasn't very forthcoming about her situation, so we'll just have to wait to see how it unfolds." Elise turned toward the Houston skyline where glass, brass and mirrored high-rises pierced the clouds. "If only we could figure out a way to grow roses at this height."

The sadness in Elise's voice surprised Nina. And the fact that she took time to muse about flowers when she seemed so like those buildings. Imposing, impressive, and impenetrable. She looked at Nina. "So, all the information is on the tickets. If you have no need for the extra ticket, I'm sure someone in the office would be happy to take it."

"No . . . no, I have someone in mind for the other ticket," she said. Aretha would love a free night out. "And thank you." She hoped she sounded genuine. Nina might be disgruntled, but she didn't want to be impolite. Seeing the worn heel on her shoe when she crossed her legs while she spoke reminded Nina she was not only going to be a stranger to covering benefits, her present wardrobe would surely mark her as a misfit. She returned both feet to the floor, hid her untidy cuticles in her lap, and exposed her fashion-sense handicap. "Is what I should wear on the ticket? Because if it's not, what do you suggest —"

"It's Black Tie Optional." She leaned in closer. Elise must have noticed her expression of confusion. "For you that means a cocktail dress or dressy separates. Some women wear long dresses, but they look like they were lost on the way to their high school prom."

Note to self: Ask Aretha if my one long dress can be shortened to cocktail length.

She stood and shuffled a stack of papers, "If you have any questions, let Tammie know."

"Yes, yes I will." Nina stood and felt the flap of her dress turn east instead of west. She smoothed it back into place. "Thank you, again. And I'm sorry that you won't be able to attend that night."

Elise looked up from her iPhone, and her eyebrows lifted as if Nina had just said something amusing. "Oh, Peyton and I will be there. But I certainly wouldn't attempt to cover the event."

6

"You know, you're not the date of my dreams."

Hearing Nina's voice, Manny whined from inside his portable pet carrier. If Aretha had been along, she could have translated. But Nina was pretty sure he'd be complaining about not riding in one of those hot, new car seats where he could sit high and view the road.

"I can't wear a pet booster seat to a fancy party, so your ride will have to wait. Besides, spending my Saturday taking you to Dr. Alvarez isn't what I had in mind for an outing either." Nina looked in her rearview mirror as she spoke, though all she could see was a pair of wet brown eyes through the netting of his carrier.

No comment from Manny. The more Nina talked to him, the more she understood the conversations between him and Aretha. Manny made for the perfect chat mate when all she needed was to net feel crazy speaking out loud when she was alone or to be able to vent because she didn't want someone to solve her problems, just to listen to them. She wasn't so sure he was as thrilled with the arrangement, but the fact that he couldn't tell her whether he was or not made him such a great non-conversationalist.

She found a parking spot on the dog side of the veterinary clinic. When she first opened the clinic, Dr. Alvarez had one common waiting room. Some of the cats would practically leap on their owners' heads when the dogs howled and growled and barked. Over time, her dog and cat clients were becoming as antagonistic as their pets. So, for everyone's safety and sanity, each now had a separate entrance. The reception desk in the center of the clinic with a swinging door on each side provided, as Dr. Alvarez said in her newsletter, ". . . just enough space for the two and four-legged creatures to get along."

After checking in, she found a corner away from the sneezing Pomeranian and the Labrador Retriever that wanted to smell every inch of her body. Nina didn't mind the wait so much. The clinic smelled like lemon oil and appeared freshly scrubbed every time she came in. In fact, the one negative about it was that it made her feel guilty about the state of the dust bunnies at her own home.

A few pages into the latest issue of *People,* it was Manny's turn. Nina always smiled when the assistant called out, "Manny O'Malley." She wasn't sure Manny was impressed by his lyrical name.

After weighing Manny and showing them to the examination room, Wendy explained to Nina that they'd be seeing the relief veterinarian because Dr. Alvarez's husband surprised her with a weekend getaway for their anniversary. "The entire office helped him plan it. He's such a romantic." Wendy hugged Manny's file to her chest and looked off into some Maui sunset. "And it doesn't hurt that he looks like a younger version of George Clooney."

"I'd be happy with the present version. Does he have an older brother?" Nina attempted to pry Manny's paws from her shoulder. He'd draped himself across her chest like a sash, and his too-long toenails dug through her sweater and into her skin. "Preferably one who doesn't mind neurotic pets." Aretha might have added "women" to that question, so it was probably good she had a hair appointment and couldn't make it.

Wendy tapped her chin and narrowed her eyes as if the answer to Nina's question might materialize if she squinted hard enough. "You know. I'm not sure. I don't remember Dr. Alvarez —"

"I was kidding, really," Nina reassured her in case she left in search of the family tree.

"Oh, I figured you were," she said and laughed like someone who just realized they'd missed the joke. She slid Manny's folder on the examining room table. "Here, let me help you with him." She gently tugged Manny from Nina. He fought valiantly and, though he ultimately lost, he snagged Nina's sweater in four places and scratched her shoulder.

But Manny was not to be denied. He squirmed out of Wendy's arms, landed on the floor, and tried to make a run for it. He almost succeeded, except a man wearing a white lab coat happened by, crouched down, and nabbed him just as he reached the doorway. "Well, you must be terribly excited to see me." He picked up Manny who, in the arms of someone tall and broad-shouldered, looked small and somewhat fearful to be held at such a height.

"I'm so sorry, I was just trying to . . ."

Wendy gestured toward Nina and Manny.

"I understand," he said and actually sounded as if he meant it. "What's . . ." he peered under Manny's belly, "his name?"

"Manny. And she was helping in the tug-of-war he was playing with me," Nina explained wanting to reassure both Wendy and Dr. Whomever of the knife-pleated khaki slacks and starched buttoned-down shirt that she wasn't upset, even with four sizable pulls in her almost new, almost cashmere sweater. Make that Aretha's sweater.

"I'm Dr. Hernandez, the relief veterinarian for Dr. Alvarez." He handed a dutifully ashamed Manny to the assistant and asked her to keep him company on the examination table. "What a relief, right?"

Nina suspected he used that line often, but she smiled anyway as if it was the most charming statement she'd heard all day. He seemed so familiar, but, after years of interviews and going through photos, everyone looked like someone she knew. Or everyone she knew looked like someone. "Nina O'Malley. Manny's mother. Of sorts."

Dr. Hernandez shook Nina's hand, but it was one of the most distracted handshakes she'd ever experienced. He might have been mentally reviewing his agenda for the day because he didn't so much look at her as he did past her, and he seemed to run out of energy. A strange slow-motion handshake. But it did have the advantage of giving her time to notice that even with a polite smile, a dimple appeared in his chin. And directly underneath it, as if drawn for emphasis, was the thin line of a scar.

"Nice to meet you," he said, but he spoke as if coming out of a brain fog.

He walked over to the table and started by checking Manny's teeth and gums. Nina hoped he wasn't going to suggest flossing because brushing his teeth required a Sumo-wrestler hold. Manny didn't mind the vaccine, but he resented his blood being drawn for the heartworm test. Nina knew this because he made the same low rumble in his throat when she'd take his squeeze toys away. Dr. Hernandez handed the blood sample to Wendy, who left the room to pass it off to someone else, Nina assumed, because she returned before Manny had finished having his temperature taken. Mortified by the indignity of the thermometer, Manny curled himself into a circle on the table. Nina scratched his head, but he didn't move. *Probably giving me the silent treatment,* Nina thought.

Dr. Hernandez checked Manny's throat,

and Nina waited to see if he'd model the open-mouthed "Ah" when he used the tongue depressor. He didn't. "Dr. Alvarez noted he's allergic to beef, so he's on potato and duck food. How's that working out for him?"

"For him, great. For me, not so much at over a dollar a can," Nina said.

He asked Wendy if the clinic had samples of the food Manny ate while he appeared to be pummeling Manny's chest and stomach.

Nina cringed. She hadn't meant to sound as if she needed a subsidy. "Wendy, don't worry about samples. I'm not struggling. Really. It's fine. I've never owned a pet before, so I didn't even know dogs had food allergies."

"Wow. Your first pet," Wendy said, politely not saying the "at your age" that was clear in her tone. "Were your parents allergic to them?"

No, they were allergic to emotional attachments. Nina shrugged. "I doubt it. My brother always wanted a Yellow Lab. He probably would've been a great vet."

"Really? So what does he do instead?" Wendy held Manny still while Dr. Hernandez poked and prodded.

Nina hated this moment because she knew her words would smack people on the blind-

60

sides of their hearts.

"Um, nothing. He died ten years ago." As she anticipated, Wendy and Dr. Hernandez exchanged those glances of shared awkwardness. She expected, when he started to speak to her that it would be the standard apology. She'd learned it helped to ease their discomfort if she preempted. So, she said, "It's okay. You didn't know. I understand."

He looked confused, not appeased. "Wait. I thought I had seen you before or at least met you someplace, but I couldn't get the memory to connect. You're Thomas's sister?"

Nina flinched. She hadn't been called Thomas's sister in over ten years. In fact, she barely knew or remembered any of his friends. "Yes. How did you know?"

"He worked with a friend of my father's who owned a construction company, Rick Higgins. I didn't know him, really, just knew he painted for Rick because they did some work around our house and the medical office." Dr. Hernandez sat on the stool near the counter, scribbled in Manny's chart, then looked at Nina as if she'd just walked in to the room. "And, I guess you don't remember me from high school, though,

61

until now I didn't totally remember you either."

"I'm going to check the inventory for those samples now," Wendy said and darted out the door.

High school? The worst four years of her teens? Nina pushed up the sleeves of her sweater and wished paper fans were still popular. But she'd have to swallow it to cool off the flush she felt radiating from her self-consciousness. All she wanted was a simple trip to the veterinarian for Manny's check-up, not a family reunion or any reunion, especially high school. She rifled through her high school yearbook in her brain, but she didn't remember graduating with anyone with his last name. "No, I'm sorry. The best part of high school was graduating."

He closed the manila file, slipped his pen in his top pocket, and rubbed the top of Manny's head. "I was three years ahead of you. That day in the cafeteria near where my friends and I sat, we weren't very nice —"

The memory exploded, sending images showering through her brain like shrapnel. "You're right. You weren't." She forgot her lunch at home, so she ate in the cafeteria that day. She hated eating there because where you sat defined your social status, and she had nowhere to go but the corner of the room. Which meant passing everyone she was invisible to. She had walked fast, so fast that she didn't see whatever was on the floor until she was on the floor with it. She had managed not to fall flat on her back, but the red divided tray dumped its entire contents into her lap. From the waist down, her jeans were splatter painted with mashed potatoes, gravy, meatloaf, and a smattering of corn. And she had just provided front row entertainment for the basketball team table.

And Greg Hernandez was their center.

7

As most significant events in Greg Hernandez's life, this too began with a phone call. This one from his sister. And, like most phone calls from his bossy older sister, this one began with her attempting to make up his mind for him.

"You need to move to Houston."

"Why? We're fine where we are. Plus, I don't have a job in Houston. I'm too young to retire and too old to live with my sister." While he talked, Greg finished loading the dishwasher, turned off the kitchen light, and stretched out on the sofa.

"You're incredibly stubborn. You must have inherited that from your father's family," Elise said.

Technically, Elise was his half-sister. She was not yet five when her father died in an oil rig accident and almost eight when her mother Beth married Greg's father, a pediatrician. Elise's pediatrician. Between the settlement from the oil company and Sidney Hernandez's income, they lived more than comfortably. Elise lived on the side of "more than," while Greg stayed content in comfortable. When their parents died on American Airlines Flight 11, the plane flown into the North Tower of the World Trade Center, Elise and Greg were forever changed. They came to realize that without one another and without the promises of a loving God, they might not have survived the tragedy themselves.

"No, I'm thinking it's a maternal trait." The sofa cushion seemed lumpier than usual. Greg reached underneath and rescued two cloth dolls, one of which was in dire need of clothes. "Look, you find me a job, and I'll start packing."

"Game on," she said.

He should have known better than to challenge Elise. A slow economy and his resistance weren't going to intimidate a woman who built a magazine from the ground up. He turned the volume back up on the television and, before he fell asleep, made a mental note to start looking for boxes.

"I'm not sure I can leave this house," Greg said, his voice heavy as he stood in his bare family room. The only evidence of a life there was the indentations in the carpet from the legs of their couch and tables.

Amelia, his next-door neighbor, held his daughter's hand and reached up with her other arm to hug him. She had been a mother to him and a grandmother to Jazarah, especially this last year. "I know, sweetie. But your memories go with you. And think how much love resonates in those walls that will bless whoever lives there."

Six years of love seeped through the pores of these walls. The arguments, he hoped, fell through the cracks of the concrete floors. Last night he walked through every room before going next-door to spend the night at Dale and Amelia's house. Lily, taking a cake out of the oven, her freckled face dewy and smiling. Lily, walking through the back door after weeding the garden, grass and dirt still visible on her bare knees. Lily, painting the nursery, her denim overalls and hair sprinkled with every color she rolled on the wall. Lily, on nights he'd work late, waiting for him, turning back the covers on his side of the bed and inviting him in with, "I missed you."

Sometimes her scent would catch him by surprise, and he would turn to look for her, his heart racing at the thought of her softness in his arms. Nights that Jazarah awoke, her screams throbbing in his chest, he rocked and cried silent tears with her. Lily was never coming home.

The next morning, Greg buckled his daughter in her car seat, hugged Amelia and Dale one more time, and looked out his rearview mirror until their waves and his home became specks and disappeared. He stopped only once on the way out of New Orleans. When he did, he unbuckled Jazarah and handed her the bundle of lilies he'd cut from their garden. "Let's go talk to Mommy," he said and took his daughter's hand.

Together they walked into Lakelawn Cemetery.

In the six months he'd been back in Houston, Greg had more requests for relief work than there were hours in the day to fill. At first, adjusting to different veterinary practices was challenging, but as his reputation grew, the doctors who hired him knew exactly what kind of service he could provide. He had the freedom to set his own schedule, be selective about the jobs he chose, and get a feel for where he might want to settle in at a practice one day.

Today he was headed to Tessa Alvarez's clinic early, since it was his first time to work there. Houston traffic, he learned, had a life all its own, and until he could take its pulse, he didn't want to risk being late.

Greg pulled into the parking lot with more than thirty minutes to spare, but since her clinic was at the front of a new residential community, he'd have time to check out the neighborhood.

He grabbed his briefcase, locked the car door, and walked around the outside of the clinic. The white-planked building with its dark green shutters and its wide wraparound porches reminded him of an Acadian home. Even the landscaping avoided the appearance of a commercial building, with curved walkways and bench areas. If the exterior of the practice was this meticulously groomed, then Greg felt sure the interior would be as well. Always reassuring because he'd worked in practices that truly had gone to the dogs.

He'd just taken a few steps when he heard the xylophone ring tone on his cell phone, which meant Paloma, the nanny was calling. Elise hired her to start the day Greg and Jazarah arrived in Houston. "She needs to be a part of your daughter's life here from the beginning. Otherwise, that's one more adjustment Jazarah needs to make." She was right. Having Paloma's help with all the logistics of moving made the transition so much smoother. Greg did tell Elise that she had to find a two-unit condo because he didn't want Paloma living in the same house, setting up an awkward and potentially problematic arrangement.

It took a great effort to not stop breathing when Greg saw her number on his cell phone. He was so afraid that she would be calling with terrible news. It was never that. This morning she called to ask if she and Jazarah could go to the zoo and the Children's Museum. "On one condition. You have to take pictures," he answered, knowing Paloma already made every event a photo op.

"She asks if she can talk to you."

"Sure. Put the princess on," he said and smiled picturing his daughter's little apple-round face, her corkscrew curls dancing when she nodded, and her bright eyes that seemed to hold their own laughter. Lily had insisted they keep her Ethiopian name, which meant "beloved princess" because, she'd said, "Isn't that what she is to us already?" How could Greg argue with that?

"Da-de? I going to the zoo," she said, her voice rising and falling with each syllable. "See what I wear?"

They'd have to start making face-to-face calls because she thought holding the phone in front of her outfit would be enough for him to see it. At first, he'd tried explaining to her that he couldn't, but it only served to frustrate her. Incredibly, she did what most adults would do in the same situation. She repeated, "See!" louder and louder, until he would finally tell her she looked adorable.

"You are beautiful," he told her, and he didn't need to see her to know it was true.

"Tank you. Talk to P now. Bye!"

Greg heard Jazarah giggling as she handed the phone off to Paloma.

"Do you want I should feed J her supper?"

His daughter and her nanny were on a first initial basis since they met. He expected his name might change to D at any time. "Yes, go ahead and do that since the clinic doesn't close until six. I'll call as soon as I'm on my way in case I don't make it home before her bedtime."

"You have a good day. We will see you later."

After every conversation with Paloma, Greg uttered a silent prayer of thanks for this young woman being in his daughter's life. Over the past year, his prayers were not always of gratitude. Actually, some of his conversations with God were rants of anger and despair and pain. He learned, though, that he could find comfort in the arms of a

God who knew grief. He didn't subscribe to the theory that God took Lily away from them. A drunk driver, with two previous arrests, took Lily on her way home from shopping for Jazarah's birthday party. God was giving her back to him, in memories, and his daughter, and the promise that he would see her again.

Manny, now on his leash, high-stepped out of the examination room with Nina following close behind. Neither one of them looked back. He wouldn't have either in her shoes.

Thomas O'Malley's sister. What a random collision in the universe of coincidence. Especially since she was the first person he'd seen from his high school since returning to Houston, and she was the last person he would have paid attention to when they were students. He had been a different Greg Hernandez then. Privileged and popular. He and his friends thought they ruled the school. They barely noticed girls like Nina. Girls who paid attention to the teacher and not them during class. Girls who did their homework and passed tests because they weren't partying all weekend. Greg and his friends pitied their sad lives.

Nina had looked familiar in that way that

a stranger appears, but your brain can't access the file of recognition. Sometimes, days later the connection happens, sometimes, not at all. Had Nina not mentioned her brother's name, Greg was certain the connection would have short-circuited before ever leading to her. He'd seen her only a few times in the hall before that day she landed on the floor and became a human food tray. Had there been a class superlative for Most Ordinary, Nina would have won. Her hair must have been long because she wore it pulled back from her round, clean-scrubbed face. She wore jeans and sweats, shirts that might have even been Thomas's. Instead of disguising her figure, the baggy clothes just magnified it.

One of his friends remarked that she might not have fallen if she hadn't been waddling so fast. That day and for days after, he and his friends would quack when they passed her in the hall. Greg knew her brother had died. He knew her family lived more than modestly. But why would he have told his friends that? They'd think he was soft. His friend Lance said she must really be a duck because all their torments seemed to roll right off her back. They grew bored and moved on.

Now, all these years later, Nina was no

longer a lump of coal in a room full of diamonds. She had become a gem herself.

But Greg also knew that transformation happens only one way.

Under extreme pressure.

8

"Shouldn't Mr. Manny be the one barking and growling coming back from the veterinarian? Sounds like you should've had a shot yourself. Distemper, maybe?" When Manny spotted Aretha, blockaded on the sofa again, he dashed across the room and tried to jump through the wall of magazines. "Of course you're glad to see me. What happened to Miss Grumpy, huh?" She set one of the stacks on the floor, so Manny would have just enough space to land on her lap.

"I won't even mention the traffic," said Nina as she set the case of special diet dog food on the counter. She dropped her purse on the floor, opened the refrigerator and slid food around looking for a bottle of water. "Do we have any —"

"In the door. Always in the door," Aretha said. "So, what happened? You look like you tangled with somebody."

Nina found two aspirins at the bottom of

her purse and washed them down. "And how's that?" She moved to the bookshelf and poured some of her water in the exhausted-looking ivy plant.

"I won't even mention the aspirins," Aretha noted in an almost-perfect mimic of Nina. She nudged Manny off her lap and settled him next to her. He thanked her with a hand lick. "You know I hate when you do that," she said and wiped the back of her hand on her jeans. "Back to you." She pointed at Nina. "I know by now when you're in a snit. Your whole face is wound tighter than Lady GaGa's clothes, your eyebrows bear down on your eyes, and your mouth does this funny fish thing." She demonstrated a pucker that made her look like a wild-haired guppy.

For a moment, Nina attempted to maintain her indignant demeanor. But the expression on Aretha's face broke her resolve, and she laughed so loudly that Manny barked at her. "If only I'd taken a picture of that, I'd have leverage for life," Nina said. "But, thanks, I needed to laugh." She cut the plastic wrap off the dog food and as she put the cans away, started telling Aretha the story of meeting Greg Hernandez, omitting what most infuriated her: the fact that the lanky high school teenager with the toothpaste-commercial smile had grown into an even more attractive version of himself.

"What a fool . . . how can someone so mean be taking care of . . . what is the matter with him?" A flustered Aretha was an incoherent Aretha. Nina learned to fill-in-the-blanks as she spoke.

"Good questions. I didn't know him in high school. I just knew of him. I mean everyone did. Everyone knows the kids with money, and everyone wants to go after the ones who are eye-candy. He was both, and he played sports. A triple play or threat depending." Nina moved to the chair in the den. "Next to losing Thomas, that day in high school was one of the worst days of my life. I wished I could have stayed on that cafeteria floor until the bell ended lunch and everyone left for class." Her mind rewound to that teenaged Nina, moving in slow motion as she stood, scraps of food clinging to her jeans. She'd bent down to pick up the tray, and her glasses slid off her face into the mess on the floor in front of her. "Getting out of there was like trying to get out of a net. The more I struggled, the deeper I sank."

"Didn't anyone try to help you?"

Aretha's outrage only magnified for Nina

now how pathetic a figure she must have been then.

"No. Well, I don't know for sure because I didn't turn around. I walked straight out through the delivery entrance."

"I bet your mother wanted to beat every one of them," said Aretha.

"I'm not sure. I never told her what really happened." Nina slipped her feet back into her ballet flats. "You're the first person I've ever shared this story with."

"You could come with me. Manny would be fine in his crate for a few hours." Nina looked down at her dog, and she didn't like what she thought she heard. "Like you know the difference between Sunday and Monday," she said to him.

He pranced off and jumped on the chair opposite where Aretha sat, using a pillow as a laptop desk, her legs crossed underneath. "I have to finish this paper, plus I have that meeting tonight."

Nina tied her neck scarf. "Meeting? On Sunday?" She looked in the mirror, muttered, and re-tied it.

"I told you about it, but you don't listen to anything that involves the word 'church.' Our women's group is deciding on our community outreach. We're just yakking over dinner." She winked at Manny, then said to Nina, "You could come with me."

"Not any more likely than you doing the same." She loosened the scarf. "Do I look like I'm wearing a neck brace? Tell me now because if you don't, she will."

"I like it. It softens you."

"So, are you saying my face looks hard?" Nina looked in the hall tree mirror, turning her head side-to-side. "Is my eyeliner too severe?"

"Sister, you are exhausting. That's not what I'm sayin' and you need to get over yourself. Just because you've revved up your career engine doesn't mean you start rolling over your friends."

"Sorry. Sorry. I have Sunday-dinner anxiety."

Aretha eyed Manny as she opened her laptop. "Well, now that's your own fault for saying 'yes' when you mean 'no.' "

To avoid thinking about the torture that awaited her, Nina shut off her usual driving music and started planning the stories that would land her in New York. The one she was putting together now had potential. If a local county official was sabotaging how contracts were being awarded, that had legs. And, with some digging, maybe even arms.

When it came to graft in government, she had to follow the roots and figure out who was on the other end. And if the ambulance service contract truly did turn out to be a political favor, that meant the mayor was willing to risk the lives of everyone in the county to stay in the good old boy network.

She'd have to be careful with documenting, verifying sources, and corroborating evidence. If the hard-hitting story came back and hit the magazine hard because of sloppy work, Elise would not be happy, and Nina could stop worrying about New York because her career would be in the dumpster. *No kids, no husband, not even a hint of one. Now's the time to make the push.*

Still no word from Daisy, which continued to concern her. That and knowing if she didn't return, Nina would be stuck going to that benefit. She had Daisy's number. It's not like she couldn't call her. But if she wasn't contacting Nina because that "it" was serious, then Daisy didn't need to be fielding calls either.

Nina exited the freeway that led to her parents' neighborhood. At least they moved to a town outside of Houston that didn't have a weapons buy-back program every other month like where they used to live. They bought a garden home, about which her mother complained to the point of calling the real estate company and threatening to sue for false advertising. "Six bushes and a tree aren't a garden. I have a throw rug bigger than the back yard," and on and on and on. When the real estate agent offered to send over boxes, movers, a for sale sign, and promised they could have them out in under twenty-four hours, she stopped the phone calls. After that, she blamed her husband and her daughter for moving her someplace she couldn't plant a decent-sized shrub.

By the time she parked in the driveway, there were enough knots in her stomach for a hammock, which, clearly, would not fit in the backyard. As always, she rang the doorbell. It sounded more like a cattle prodder on steroids. Nina fiddled with her scarf, dusted off the threat of something she might not have seen on the front of her emerald green silk dress, and checked the toes of her platform shoes for scuffs. She swiped her front teeth with her finger in case of lipstick bleed and hoped she'd brushed her teeth without leaving anything behind.

She heard her mother's, "I'll get it," as if battling her father to open the door was ever an issue. Sheila O'Malley peered out like she might be expecting a deep cover agent for an exchange.

"Oh, it's you. Well, come on in. But you're early. Dinner isn't ready yet. Just make yourself at home."

Right. It's what she'd been trying to do her entire life.

9

Nina wondered if all grown children, when they looked at their parents through adult eyes, tried to find what first attracted them to one another. She'd seen all the old photos paraded around the house that captured smiles meant for the camera. But it was what happened before and after the picture that intrigued Nina. If she could travel back in time to show the young Patrick O'Malley, the one with the dimples and broad smile, whose eyes signaled mischief and zest, a photo of what he would become in forty years, might something in his life have changed? Maybe so much so that the Patrick O'Malley, who now waved his remote like a king's scepter from the throne of his recliner, the one whose downturned eyes matched his downturned mouth, whose hair was gray and disheveled, might have been someone else? Or perhaps Nina might not have been at all?

"When did you get here?" He made motions as if he was going to disengage himself from the comfort of his chair.

Oh, almost thirty years ago. "Don't get up," she said and walked over to kiss him on his forehead. He smelled just like the closed-up insides of an unhappy house. "How are you?"

"Good. Good." He spoke to the cast of *Gilligan's Island* on the television screen. "You?"

Awful. My career is off-the-tracks, my social life consists of taking my dog to the veterinarian, only to meet the one jerk I've tried to forget for the past ten years. "I'm great. Everything's great."

"Glad to hear that, honey." His eyes flickered in her direction for a moment. "Your mom need some help in the kitchen?"

Sheila didn't need help in the kitchen, the house, the country, the universe. Had he forgotten Nina trailing behind him during those years when he spent more time vertical? She'd hand him tools when he fixed the leaky something or other under the car, tape when he bundled the outside pipes against the cold. He didn't need help either, but he at least let her think he did. And Nina loved him for that.

"Doubt it, but I'll check." She wasn't sure

he knew she left.

Nina walked through the hall to the kitchen where she would be of no help whatsoever. For someone whose idea of an emotional moment was sneezing, Sheila created lovely meals. Given the choice, Nina would have preferred peanut butter and jelly sandwiches if that meant her mother could invest more time in her.

Sheila hated hovering, so Nina leaned against the doorway between the kitchen and the dining room. Aretha would be in designer heaven if given the chance to makeover the industrial look of the kitchen with its stainless steel appliances, gray tiled floors, and white cabinets. But her mother puttering around a French country kitchen wearing a cornflower blue apron edged in lace was as likely as Madonna showing up at an award ceremony wearing a cotton housedress and slippers. "Smells great in here. Anything I can do?"

Her mother sprinkled sliced almonds on top of a salad. "No. Not now. Everything's almost finished." She sighed. "I've been in here all morning making lasagna while your dad's been in there," she nodded her head toward the den, "wearing out the batteries in the remote."

"I would have been glad to be here sooner

to help you," Nina said and hated that she felt like a child uninvited to a party.

"All you had to do was offer." Sheila lifted that one eyebrow that signaled "so there," as she added olive oil and vinegar to the salad.

Nina shoved her indignation away before it jumped right out of her mouth and splat itself on her mother's forehead. Instead, it coursed through her body and, if someone had struck a match, Nina would have exploded on the spot.

After Thomas died, the fourth chair at the dining table screamed his absence. It screamed so loudly that for months and months and months, Nina and her parents took refuge in the den where they balanced their plates on television tables and finished their meals in communal silence. Nina looked across the table now at Thomas's empty chair and between the clicks of forks against the thick white plates, wondered what he would have been like at almost forty. Would they have expanded their table for Thomas, his wife, their children? She almost hoped he couldn't see them all now. See how they all went on living, but died inside.

"So, how's that writing job of yours?"

Even with one eye on the television, at least her father pretended an interest in her career. However, when her mother figured out that her daughter wasn't going to be Houston's version of *Entertainment Tonight,* Sheila thought Nina had just wasted her college education. After Janie's promotion, it frightened Nina that, once again, her mother might be right.

Nina started to explain the story about the mayor and his cronies when her mother interrupted to ask if she had a life outside of that job.

"Yes, of course." She didn't add that it mostly centered around Manny. "In fact, Elise, my editor gave me tickets to the We Care benefit. The one that's held at the St. Regis Hotel."

"That fancy one the Houston society people go to? Isn't it an AIDS thing? And who are you going with?"

Her mother hadn't asked her that many questions in the past four dinners they shared. "Since the tickets cost $400 each, I imagine it's going to be an upscale crowd. As for the 'AIDS thing,' the money raised at the benefit goes to local hospices. There's also a silent auction of quilts made by different support groups in Houston. I read online there's going to be a display of a sec-

86

tion of The AIDS Memorial Quilt."

"Seems like if everyone's paying that much money to attend, you'd be able to see the whole quilt," her father observed and served himself another slab of lasagna.

"Well, I've done some research. The quilt is not very portable anymore. It weighs fifty-four tons. The article said if you spend just a minute on one panel, it would take over thirty-three days to see the entire thing. I don't think anyone can stay that long," said Nina.

Neither of her parents laughed. Her mother's lips twisted to the side, which Nina learned in her teens was a prelude to a lecture on being sassy. Her father's head bobbed and a thin thread of cheese hung from his lips. He looked like an aging redfish that had just swallowed a hook. *And just think, Thomas, you missed all this.*

Sheila handed her husband a napkin. "You need to take care of that," she said and pointed to her chin to demonstrate. She looked at Nina. "What are you going to do with that extra ticket? Have someone in mind? Because if you don't, Lola across the street told me she has a son who isn't married yet. He owns three fast food restaurants, and he makes a good income." She stretched the word "good" to two syllables.

87

"Then why is he still single?" Lola must be the new neighbor her mother mentioned last month. The one whose furniture didn't arrive via a moving van, but through a convoy of local furniture store delivery trucks.

Her mother patted her mouth with her napkin as if her lips would shatter if she pressed them too hard, cleared her throat, and smiled too deliberately for Nina's comfort. "Well, funny you should ask that because Lola asked the same about you."

Not staying for the key lime pie her mother had made shaved about thirty minutes off Nina's torture time. She rarely ate dessert there anyway because it was usually something she didn't like. Since her mother's eyes seemed to focus on Nina's hips each time she offered her something sweet, she guessed her refusing it was her mother's plan all along. Either that or her mother purposely provided her an easy escape.

The sound of Nina's key in the deadbolt flipped an internal barking switch in Manny that didn't shut off until he spotted her walking through the door.

"I need to remind your human grandmother there's at least one man in my life who can't contain his excitement when I walk through the door." Manny's tail wagged like a windshield wiper as he wiggled out of his crate and into Nina's arms. "Though you really do need to chew a few breath mints before you tell me hello."

Manny trotted up the stairs after Nina. He gnawed on a rawhide bone he found under her bed, while she changed into her sweats. She rifled through her closet hoping to find something she already knew wouldn't be there: a dress to wear to the benefit. Nothing even close to benefit-worthy. That dress she hoped Aretha could modify would set off the fashion police alarm.

"Aretha doesn't know it yet, but there's a shopping trip in her future," Nina told Manny as she grabbed her laptop from her dresser. He paid no attention to her until she mentioned going downstairs for food. He pushed the bone under her bed and led the way to the kitchen.

After Manny had been fed, watered, and escorted outside for his nightly routine of fertilizing the flower bed, Nina settled in her chair to read the online news and compose questions for the council member she'd soon be interviewing. She opened her email to find a message from Daisy.

"Just wanted you to know I'm fine, and I

should be back in time for Janie's party. Not much to talk about right now. I'll call you. Hugs, D."

That was all the online news Nina could handle for the night.

10

The day after Greg's unexpected reunion with Nina O'Malley, he left Dr. Alvarez's clinic and drove straight to the support group meeting he first attended four months ago. Elise, of course, found Threads of Hope even before he moved back to Houston. What she neglected to tell him was not only was this HIV/AIDS support group primarily women, they spent almost every meeting sewing quilt panels. The group, of course, knew everything about him, including the little known fact that he dabbled in photography, pencil sketches, and watercolors. All talents the group welcomed with enthusiasm, especially as they prepared their quilts for the We Care benefit.

He told his sister later that he might not have ever returned to the group had a little girl named Tabitha and The AIDS Memorial Quilt not led him and Lily to their daughter.

"Well, that worked out nicely then, didn't it?" Elise purred, and Greg saw the look of triumph blaze in her eyes.

Tonight, thinking of that exchange between himself and his sister, Greg smiled at her ability to transform what some might see as manipulative into something serendipitous. Lily would have been delighted by the group considering her gratitude to the NAMES Project Foundation for all it did to preserve and care for the quilt that they'd viewed in Syracuse, New York.

Originally, Greg hadn't planned for his wife to join him at the Syracuse veterinary conference. But when she had her third miscarriage weeks before, Greg insisted she go with him. The second day there, Lily sent him a text asking him to meet her after his sessions at the Oncenter Convention Center. He found her sitting on a bench when he arrived, writing in the small leather-bound journal she carried in her purse. Though she smiled when she spotted him and her eyes were dry, he knew she'd been crying because of the faint, uneven black smudges under her lower lashes.

"I want to show you something," was all she'd said when she'd reached for his hand and led him into the center where huge quilts rained from the ceiling. Lily could barely thread a needle, so he couldn't understand what might have attracted her to a quilters' convention display. Reading the question his face asked, Lily explained the quilts were all panels from the larger AIDS Memorial quilt, on display there because the first day in December was World AIDS Day.

Without offering any more in the way of explanation, she said, "Come see this," and brought him through the exhibit to a quilt on the far right end. She pointed to a cotton-candy pink panel, edged in white lace and seeded all over with beads that looked like pearls. A buttercup yellow crocheted bonnet, a smocked dress that looked as if it had been dipped in the sky the blue was so delicate, a silver teething ring that bore the tiniest of indentations, and a lace bib that barely showed signs of use were all attached to the panel. In the center of the quilt, the name Tabitha was embroidered in white thread. Underneath, in the same embroidered script, was "Age: 5 months when she went to the Lord in peace."

Continuing to stare at the panel, she said, "Do you know that about one thousand babies are born with HIV every day?"

"No. I didn't know that," he responded,

sure that until today, Lily probably didn't know that either. Greg looked down at his wife and wondered if this experience was healthy for a woman mourning another failed pregnancy.

She turned to him. "And half of them will die before their second birthday without treatment."

"That's a staggering number," he said. Instead of unsure, Greg now felt uneasy. Lily's plane was coming in for a landing, but he still couldn't locate the runway. When she informed him that 90 percent of the world's HIV infected children live in Africa, Greg knew the wheels had hit the ground. A year later, Greg and Lily traveled over eight thousand miles, and this time when the plane landed, they were the parents of a solemn-eyed baby girl.

Later, Lily would tell anyone with ears that losing three babies due to miscarriages brought them to another one. She never doubted that God meant for them to be Jazarah's parents. And Greg never doubted Lily's absolute conviction. He already felt blessed to be loved by Lily. Knowing their little daughter would be loved so fiercely and generously, how could he say anything but yes?

Tonight, that little girl was tucked into

bed under her princess blanket, her head on her princess pillowcase, and slept unaware that 99 percent of the HIV in her body was undetectable. And while she slept, Greg and the rest of the support group he'd be meeting at the Fellowship Hall planned to put the finishing touches on the two quilts they would be donating for auction at the benefit.

Nina showed Aretha the email from Daisy. "What do you think this means?" In the time she waited for her roommate to return, Nina exhausted every possibility she could think of.

"You really want to know?" Aretha sipped her tea, set her cup down, and eyed Nina. "It means she's fine, you're not, and when she's ready to tell you something, she will. Oh, and she'll be back for Janie's party."

"Wow. What did you eat for dinner? Nails?" Nina closed her laptop.

"You asked me. So don't start playing your mother by asking me questions that you already have the answer to."

"That was harsh, too. What's going on?" Nina regretted ever beginning the conversation.

Aretha tossed the rubber ball that Manny just nosed in her direction. "I'm telling you this because I care about you —"

"Stop right there. It's late, and I'd rather you just get to the point instead of dancing all around whatever it is you want me to hear."

"Then, here it is, girlie. Ever since Brady stopped calling and Janie announced her promotion, you've dragged your face around here. Then, when Daisy didn't show up for work, your first thought wasn't about her well-being. You dove into the conspiracy theory and barely came up for air. Now, you're determined to break the political story of the year to get Elise's attention." Aretha added more hot water to her tea. "I guess if you believed that God had another plan for you, you might not be so bitter."

Nina snickered. "God has another plan for me? Why? Did He finally figure out this one wasn't working? Let's see, my only brother died, I spent all of high school trying to make my lumpy self invisible, the only relationship my mother and I share is our mutual disappointment in me, and my father is buried so deep inside that shell of himself I don't know if there's a shovel long enough to reach him." Manny jumped on the chair and draped himself across her lap. "So, are you telling me God's not in favor of my wanting to make a career move?"

"I don't pretend to know what God

knows. What I do know is that you see New York as some geographical cure for your life. Maybe God's giving you what you need right here, but you just can't see it."

"Enlighten me," said Nina, exasperation evident in her voice.

"Elise could have given those benefit tickets to someone else in the office. Really, how difficult is it to cover an 'ooh-la-la' event with all the beautiful people? Someone could probably look up the one last year, change a few names, and — *voilà* — instant coverage. Maybe Elise wants to see what you're going to do with something you believe is mundane."

"Oh, so you're thinking this is some kind of test? God's or Elise's?"

Aretha placed her cup and saucer in the sink. "That's exactly what I think, and whose test it might be doesn't matter. So far, you've not even shown up for it."

11

"Dr. Hernandez is here. Hide the cookies, Miss Martha."

"You mean you haven't eaten them all already?" Greg tousled Jacob's hair on the way to the coffee pot in the Fellowship Hall. Not yet twelve, Jacob and his six-year-old sister Helen were adopted from Ethiopia four years ago. When his parents died, Jacob was seven and, until social workers came to their home, he had been taking care of his sister Helen by himself. Now the siblings live with their adoptive parents, Pam and Eli, and their three biological children. "Where's your Mom?" Jacob pointed over Greg's shoulder where Pam sat with three other women at a table bearing a mountain of fabrics.

"They told me to find more scissors. Guess they think I'm old enough to handle them." Jacob shook his head. "I think they're just tired of doing all the cutting themselves," he observed, then shuffled off in the direction of the supply room.

Greg smiled and looked around for Martha, the group's matriarch and founder. From the time he first met her, he felt an instant connection. She reminded him of Amelia, his neighbor in New Orleans who meant so much to both him and Jazarah. Martha walked out of the storeroom with a pair of scissors before Jacob even reached the door. "Here ya go, baby," she said as she handed him the scissors and another bag of fabric. Close to eighty, Martha told everyone she'd earned the right to call everyone else "baby." No one dared disagree, mostly out of respect. Then again, at almost six feet tall, her silver hair cropped close to her face, she made quite the imposing figure.

"Hey, Doc," she called out to Greg. She gave him a quick hug when she reached him. "Saved ya some cookies of your own to take home." She winked, then asked him to give the two quilts they were donating a final look.

"I see you're already starting on more," Greg said. "Those for next year?"

She shrugged. "We thought we'd try to get a few ready for the county fair. Plus, Becca asked if we could make one for a patient of hers. And, I know we all like to have a say in the ones for the benefit every year, but I thought it couldn't hurt to have some pieces ready. Crystal works at the Goodwill store, and she had the idea of bringing some clothes from there. We're just cutting big squares and whatnots for now."

Becca, a hospice nurse, joined the group a few months ago after seeing a quilt they'd made that belonged to one of her patients. "I may not be a seamstress," she said when she introduced herself, "but I can operate a pair of scissors and thread a needle."

Crystal and her mother Kelley were members of Living Faith church and helped the group secure the Fellowship Hall for their meetings. Crystal's twin sister, Carlys, after several trips to rehab, still couldn't stay clear of drugs. She died of AIDS when she was sixteen from a needle share. Kelley said the quilting group and just pushing a needle to create something good were all the therapy she needed since her daughter's death more than five years ago.

Greg set his coffee down before walking to the tables where the finished quilts awaited final inspection. Last year, the group had decided to make one quilt for children and one for adults. The children's quilt was designed using a pattern called

Cupcake, but they nixed using a cupcake fabric. Greg thought it might be too limiting, and despite all the gender neutral talk, he didn't think cupcakes would appeal to parents of boys. Instead, they used a fabric featuring apple green, orange, and aqua colored giraffes against a bright yellow background sprinkled with cherry red hearts. The quilt's border was a polka dot fabric of complementary colors, and edging the border were strips of yellow gingham. Greg thought he might have to bid on this one himself because his daughter loved seeing the "stretchy" giraffes as she called them, and he could already picture her giggling and pointing to the diamonds of the happy-colored animals.

Greg flipped over the bottom right corner. "Aren't we sewing one of the 'Threads of Hope' labels on the back?"

"Oops. See, you really are helpful. I'm on my way to get one, and I'll be right back," she said. She took a few steps then turned around. "Doc, best check the other one."

"This one's ready to go," he said seeing the circle logo of their group carefully stitched to the back of the double pinwheel spin patterned quilt. Though the quilt used only five different fabrics, the nine pinwheels were all sewn over the same lime green firefly-designed diamonds, which were stitched over nine snow-white squares of fabric. Two of the pinwheel arms were sewn from a hot pink fabric with red-and-lime green paisley prints. The other fabric featured a white background with hot pink added to the paisley print. Greg thought the almost retro-colored fabric and design might attract some of the younger attendees at the benefit.

Martha returned with a threaded needle and a label. "We need to write Elise a thank you note for donating all this fabric," she said as she held the quilt corner, her thumb holding the label straight while her needle flashed through the fabric.

"She doesn't expect that," Greg said.

Martha paused, cocked her head to one side, and narrowed her eyes. "Now, Doc, we're not doing it because she expects us to. We're doing it because we want to. And it's the right thing to do, to tell people you appreciate them for helping you get somewhere you need to be."

"Guess I needed to be reminded of that," he said, thinking of the backlog of thank-you notes he should've written. Beginning with Nina who, all those years ago in high school, started him on his journey toward compassion. And Lily who traveled the road with him. And Jazarah for bringing it to life.

Nina stepped into the elevator and stared straight into the eyes of Brady Lambert. "What . . . how . . . why are you here?" *At least I'm incoherent when no one else is here.* Before she could step aside, he reached around to press the button for their floor. His arm grazed hers and she caught a wisp of his familiar Dolce & Gabbana woody-citrus scent.

"Hmm. I still work here, right?" He shifted his black leather camera bag just as Nina attempted to sidestep him. But, too late. The bag hit her cup, and launched a spray of foam and coffee. Some of it splashed on Nina's pumps, but Brady's grey cable-knit sweater soaked up the rest.

"Thanks. What a great way to start my day," he said and glared at the half-dry napkin Nina offered him as if she just pulled it out of a baby's diaper.

She was just about to tell him that he should be glad the cup was half full, and he needed to be more careful swinging heavy camera bags in small spaces when the doors opened on their floor. Brady had a foot out the door before it had opened all the way. He pulled his cell phone out of his pants pocket and, as he left the elevator, turned to Nina and said, "Elise must be saving a bundle in dry-cleaning bills keeping you off the big stories."

Stunned into muteness, Nina rode the elevator right back down to the parking garage again. Fortunately, no one got on, so she had time to compose herself and think of places she could have finished off what was left of her coffee on Brady. And when did he become so snarky? And why?

When she finally made it through the office doors, Nina knew the latte aroma did as well.

Michelle raised her eyes over her reading glasses. "I've been wondering when you'd surface. Mr. Happy steamrolled in here complaining about your lack of gracefulness. He might have mentioned something about a dry cleaning bill . . ." She smiled at Nina. "Have a nice day, dearie. Ignore the malcontents."

Nina dropped her cup in the wastebasket by Michelle's desk. "The thrill is gone . . ."

"Speaking of thrills, I emailed you a few messages. Seems you're stirring the nepotism pot in that county election."

Maybe Aretha was wrong about this one. How can a quilt auction compete with election fraud? Readers want corruption exposed, not benefit dollars. Nina decided she'd postpone a discussion with Elise about her idea for an ongoing feature story about the We Care benefit and auction. If anyone understood the importance of news that mattered, it was Elise.

Nina planned to meet Aretha after work so they could shop for something to wear to the benefit. After spending most of the day talking to county officials, the District Attorney's office, more research into how contracts were awarded and to whom, Nina was ready for an afternoon that involved nothing more than, "love it/hate it." She thought they were going to start at The Galleria, but Aretha's text said to meet at a shop on Richmond.

"Why are we here?" Nina whispered to Aretha as they walked over to a rack of cocktail dresses. "I thought we were going shopping for new dresses, not used ones."

Aretha laughed. "Look at this store. Does this look like a used clothing shop?"

Nina swiveled her eyes from one end of the store to the other. Chandeliers, Oriental rugs, period furniture. "No, it doesn't. But I still don't understand what we're going to find here."

"Look, we can't compete on the same playing field as some of those divas who'll be sashaying around at that benefit. We're so not on the same playing field, we couldn't even be the water girls." Aretha scoped out the cocktail dress rack, flipping price tags as she talked. "So, we're not even going to try to play their game. Vintage clothes are classics. Just because they're old, doesn't mean they're outdated. We'll make a statement, but in a way that's unique and sophisticated. I promise."

Several racks and hours later, they each found the dress of their dreams. Aretha bought an off-shoulder, wine velvet dress with a scallop trim on the neckline, shoulders, and back. Nina's dress from the 1950s seemed to have been designed to fit her. The black taffeta dress had a polka dot illusion net bodice, cropped sheer sleeves, and a tulle skirt lining.

Nina had heard Brady might be there. She hoped so. Maybe seeing her in this dress would cause him to redefine *clumsy*.

12

"Peyton and I are about to leave. We wouldn't mind swinging by to pick you up," said Elise. "Would we?" She directed the question to her husband, who must have been in the room when she called. Peyton answered loudly enough for Greg to hear him, "I think Greg trusts that you're telling the truth."

Greg laughed. "Ask him if he wants me to pick him up instead."

"The two of you deserve one another," she said, the smirk apparent in her voice. "But the truth is, he looks so great in a tux, I think I want to walk in with a trophy husband on my arm."

"Thanks for the offer, really. I'm leaving as soon as I tuck Jazarah in."

"Give the little princess a hug and kiss from the two of us. See you soon," said Elise.

Greg tucked his phone in his pocket and

headed upstairs to his daughter's room. He knew his sister wanted him to ride to the benefit with them to spare his having to walk in alone. And he appreciated, not only that she offered, but that she didn't say the obvious. But for Greg, it wasn't just the arriving by himself that magnified Lily's absence on nights like tonight. He missed her little rituals, like when she'd lift her hair so he could zip her dress, and he'd always take the opportunity to softly kiss the back of her neck. Or when she'd spray a new perfume on the inside of her wrist, then hold it up to him to ask if he approved. And before they'd walk out the door, she'd make him stand perfectly still while she adjusted his tie, smoothed the lapels on his jacket, and declared him presentable with a soft kiss. Then she'd laugh that she'd just given him a lipstick cheek, and she'd smooth it over with her hand that was as soft as her face.

Will someone ever love me that way again? And, as he opened the door to Jazarah's room, he wondered if someone would ever love her again with Lily's fierceness and abundance. One thing he knew for sure. They were a package deal. And that was his prayer, always, that God would open his heart to a woman who would accept them both. A woman after God's own heart.

Greg tapped lightly on the partially closed door. "Is there a special little girl here?"

"Daddy, Daddy, come see!" His daughter's excitement reached him before he stepped into the room.

Paloma sat, Jazarah on her lap, in the pink-and-white ticked armchair that Jazarah called her reading chair. The small crib quilt that Lily had sewn for her while they waited for word they could finally fly to her was an uneven ball of fabric bunched in her arms. Every night Greg tucked her in with the quilt, always showing her the square that Lily stitched with, "I'll love you forever," and his daughter's sleepy eyes would blink as she'd clutch the quilt to her chest and whispered, "J woves you, too."

Jazarah waved him over and pointed to the page in Max Lucado's *You Are Special* where Eli, the woodcarver, explains to the wooden Wemmick Punchinello that the stickers the others use to label him only matter if he lets himself care about them. Greg loved the story's message, that joy comes from what God thinks of us, not others, and that in His eyes we are all special, regardless of how we look.

When he and Lily bought the book years ago, they knew their daughter would face all sorts of issues and not just because of her race. Being an HIV-positive child would not be a ticket to popularity. But what made Jazarah special was what made her different, and what made her different would make her later question her self-worth. As her parents, Greg and Lily were determined their daughter grow with the conviction that nothing could sway God from loving her. *You Are Special* became a book that they gave to their own families and many of their adult friends, some of whom apparently either forgot or were never told the message.

His daughter pointed to Paloma's face, then his, then her own. "No 'tickers!" She grinned as she clapped her hands.

"Come hug me, no sticker girl." Greg held out his arms, and she reached for him. He gathered her close with her familiar just bathed, lavender soap smell and still damp hair. "Paloma will tuck you in tonight because daddy is going to Aunt Elise's party."

Jazarah loosened her arms from around his neck and leaned back against his arms, her brown eyes targeted on his own. "Why?" Her expression, so solemn and yet so parental-like, made him want to laugh.

"Remember Daddy told you about the

party to raise money so more mommies and daddies can bring home beautiful little girls like you?"

She glanced up at the ceiling, then back at him. "Uh-huh."

Greg kissed her forehead, then settled her in Paloma's lap. "Well, that's where I'm going. I'll wake you up in the morning, and we can have pancakes for breakfast."

She grabbed her quilt and wiggled comfortably back in her reading spot. "Like me?"

He laughed. "Yes, I'll make 'J' pancakes just for you." One morning he made pancakes in an assortment of alphabet shapes, and they hadn't been round since. Unless they were the letter "O."

"Both doses, right?" Greg asked Paloma as he smoothed his daughter's hair.

She nodded. "Yes, sir. Both on time."

Even though he asked the question daily, and even though she answered the same daily, Greg appreciated that Paloma responded each time as if his daughter's required regimen of drugs was new. She knew, because of the drugs she took herself, that missing a dose of antiretroviral therapy or even juggling the times the drugs were administered were the biggest threats to HIV-positive kids. A disruption in the schedule either way could mean chancing the virus would become resistant to the therapy.

"Great. Thanks." Greg kissed his daughter one more time. "I love you, my special Wemmick."

She smiled and mashed her quilt against her chest. "Me, too. Forever and ever."

When Nina entered the Astor Ballroom of the St. Regis Hotel, every notion she had about attending a benefit of this magnitude hid in shame. And she promised herself to never roll her eyes again when someone described an event as "breathtaking." Well, perhaps if they sounded like Marilyn Monroe when they said it, she might have to reconsider.

The scene before her was spectacular. Tens of thousands of sparkling white lights canopied the ceiling. Huge spindly trees wrapped in the same white lights branched across the room and met one another. Tables were draped in subdued silver cloths of polished cotton. The tailored chair covers matched the tablecloths but were anchored to the chairs with wide white satin ribbons wrapped around the backs and tied with generous bows. Riding the waves of conversations, the stringed music of the violins and harps sailed across the ballroom.

Thanks to Aretha, she didn't feel at all uncomfortable among the couture collections that surrounded her. Brady did attend, camera in hand, and she could tell by the appraising nod when he walked past her that he didn't, at first, recognize her. Aretha told her that he turned around, took a few steps toward her, then must have changed his mind because he stopped and headed in his original direction. Nina decided that if their paths did cross again that night, she'd ask him why he wasn't in New York with Janie scouting out places to live. Between bites of steamed asparagus stems, Aretha warned her that such a question was truly none of her business. "He doesn't owe you an explanation. And even if he gives you one, I don't know why you are torturing yourself. If he says there's no more Janie, are you really interested? And if you are, don't tell me. I don't want to lose all respect for you."

Nina ignored Aretha's dire predictions. "Let's go view the quilts before the silent auction ends," she said.

"I'll meet you there. I just saw someone I want to say hello to." Aretha dashed off before Nina had a chance to find out who the someone was.

The quilts were in the adjoining room. They covered every wall and just walking around the room was like stepping inside a giant kaleidoscope with a landscape of fabrics and textures and even dimensional objects. When Elise first gave her the tickets, Nina expected that the auction would feature quilts that memorialized family or friends lost to AIDS. But it was the money raised from the event that would go toward supporting the efforts of the NAMES Project and their ongoing work with the Memorial Quilt. The ones on display that night were sewn by local support groups throughout the Houston area. Nina recognized some of the traditional quilts, classic patchworks with patterns dizzyingly intricate. Lace, beads, even trinkets embellished some of the contemporary quilts.

Nina spotted a quilt whose funky design and colors she was certain Aretha and her little decorator-self would adore. It would be a perfect birthday present for her because Nina knew that it was a luxury she wouldn't buy for herself right now. Standing in front of the hot pink and lime green paisley print quilt, Nina was the first bidder and realized she had no idea how much she should bid. She looked around for people wearing "We Care" pins, which meant they were volunteers attending the benefit to help with the auction.

A few couples moved past her, and she spotted a lapel pin on the tuxedo of a man who stopped to bid on the giraffe quilt next to her. He was still writing on the bid sheet when she tapped on his shoulder. "Excuse me. I'm sorry to bother you, but I wanted to bid on this for a friend, and I saw your lapel pin —"

When he placed his pen down on the bid sheet to look up, there was the shock of mutual recognition as Greg Hernandez and Nina O'Malley stood face-to-face.

13

Brady, she expected to see. Greg Hernandez? Not so much.

And Greg Hernandez in a tuxedo? Not so shabby. In fact, she wanted to slap herself for the flicker of warmth she was certain flushed her face. Even if she did find him surprisingly attractive, she certainly did not want him to feel even a stitch of satisfaction to see it reflected in the blush on her cheeks.

They both tripped over their words like wires stretched across their mutual discomfort at finding themselves where they would not have wanted to be.

After swatting a few syllables in one another's direction, Nina managed a coherent sentence. "I didn't know you worked here," she said. *Another deserved slap for a ridiculous comment. Aretha, anytime you want to make an appearance and save me would be fine.* She shifted her weight ever-so-slightly to give her other foot a reprieve from the tingling that led to total toe numbness and would make a speedy escape improbable. "Volunteer, I meant I didn't know you were a volunteer." What she really wanted to say was that she was stunned to find him at an event supporting anything AIDS-related.

"Well, I didn't know I was one either until a week or so ago," Greg said. "It's given me something to do and kept me out of trouble." He smiled and added, "So far."

"There you are," the voice of relief tinged with frustration, sailed above the heads of the cluster of people. It originated from a woman who snaked her way through a cluster of sequined gowns against a backdrop of black tuxedos. Her cropped platinum hair seemed as no-nonsense as the simple black sheath she wore. Nina had heard about the death of his parents, so she knew whoever this was, she wasn't his mother. Her eyes flickered on Nina for only a moment, then she handed Greg a plastic cup and a bottle of water the size and shape of a coffee thermos. "Who'd want to go hiking with that?" She emphasized *that* and pointed to the container she'd given him. "Glass water bottles? Better off putting it in a can," she harrumphed.

Greg laughed. "You're the queen of practical. Thanks for the water." He set the cup and bottle down on the table next to them. "Did you need me for anything?"

"Crystal was following me. She had a question about taking orders from people who don't win the auction." She looked over her shoulders and back at Greg. "Guess she got sidetracked." Turning her attention to Nina, she said, "You're bidding on that one? Good choice," she said and walked off.

As she threaded her way back through the crowd, Greg watched her and shook his head, an amused smile on his face. "That was Martha. Her group made that quilt. She left so quickly, I didn't have time to introduce you."

"Oh, so you've been to this benefit before?" Nina said, trying not to lick her dry lips and wondering if her breath reeked of the grilled garlic-infused cilantro shrimp she'd sampled earlier.

Two women who walked over to look at the quilt squeezed past Nina, pushing her within inches of Greg. In high school, she dreamed of being this close to him. Close enough to punch him, which she knew would have hurt her more. Physically. She contemplated other ways of marring the face that so many girls in school wanted pressed against their own. After her brother died, she abandoned what she considered the smoke and mirrors of praying to an invisible God. But the one prayer she let escape her lips was that Greg Hernandez know pain. The gut-altering pain that she experienced.

Greg twisted what, at first Nina thought was a wedding band, but the ring was on his right hand instead of his left. "No, I haven't. My sister invited me, and Martha, well . . ." He stopped, drank some water, and looked into his cup as if expecting to find the rest of his sentence there. Greg set the cup on the table and when he looked at Nina, he said, "Anyway, I doubt you're interested in a rambling narrative about how I came about being here. What about you? Were you here last year?"

Nina wished he hadn't sounded so much like a polite customer service rep, trained to ask scripted questions. *Really? This is the second time you've seen one another in years. Why are you expecting more than feigned interest?* She considered an equally vague answer, but why? What were the odds their ships would dock at the same port? Might as well go for honest. "I wasn't here before either, and the only reason I'm here tonight is because I'm on assignment. Not that I don't think this is a worthy cause, but

119

charity events, you know the who's who doing the what's what, aren't the stories I write." She moved to the side to avoid a possible collision into Greg, letting a couple holding hands and reeking of fresh love walk by. "I'd rather do more investigative reporting. But . . . my editor gave me the tickets. And, she's not someone I want to annoy by refusing. In fact, I wouldn't doubt she's the reincarnation of General Patton, the female version. She's demanding and driven, and that's as diplomatically as I can describe her."

A carousel of expressions moved over Greg's face as she spoke. From expectant to thoughtful to confused to amused. She didn't remember being humorous. Perhaps the orchestra tuning up in the ballroom lent a dramatic backdrop to her tale of woe. Otherwise, what was that flicker of a smile?

"Oh, so you're a reporter. Local news station?" He poured himself more water.

"I'd rather be behind a camera than in front of one. No, I work for a local magazine called *Trends*. You might not have seen it yet if you just recently moved."

Greg almost choked trying to swallow his water. "Excuse me," he coughed out.

Nina opened her purse to find a tissue to hand him when she heard Aretha calling

120

her. "Nina, look who I found." Her relief withered faster than a Southern girl in the Georgia sun when she looked up to see Elise trailing behind her friend. "Oh, great. Speak of the devil . . ." she said as she handed Greg the only thing she could dredge up, a napkin from Starbucks. "I'll tell her I'm interviewing you, which, of course, I planned to do next anyway, and maybe she'll march off in another direction."

He started coughing again.

If Greg had known that being a volunteer would provide him the front-row entertainment about to unfold before him, he would have signed on without his sister's persistence.

"If you're going to be there, you might as well have something to do and not wander around aimlessly," Elise had told him when she handed over his pin.

At first, he thought it was her ploy to assure that he'd show up. But walking in tonight, he realized that, by giving him a mission for the evening, she saved him from the awkwardness of feeling alone in a room full of people.

He expected to feel a bit awkward without Lily. He didn't expect that he would feel that way standing near the woman he least expected to see there. What made meeting her all the more uncomfortable was his realization that, even before he knew that he knew her, she'd captured his attention. Greg remembered thinking that only a woman as beautiful as she was self-assured would be able to pull off wearing a quirky, but stunning vintage dress to such an occasion. He would have never guessed that the girl he humiliated on the floor of his high school cafeteria would be the woman admired in the ballroom of a grand hotel.

It was reassuring that she was equally startled to see him. Of course, based on what he suspected was her perception of him — arrogant, spoiled, and unfeeling — her surprise didn't surprise him. The last time they'd seen one another was her appointment at the vet clinic with her dog, the squirmy dachshund that she'd named after some city. He didn't have a reason to discuss his daughter or his wife. Had he, she might have been less shocked.

When she started explaining her reason for being at the benefit, Greg thought her working for Elise would be too coincidental. Then, as she continued to talk, the notion became less unlikely. Describing her editor as demanding came close to Elise, but he almost couldn't stop himself from laughing aloud when she mentioned *Trends.* Then, as if on cue, his sister appeared. At first, he thought the comedy of errors would be amusing. But seeing the change in Nina's demeanor, the way she squared her shoulders and tugged on the pearl drop she wore, centering it in the hollow of her neck, he sensed a pending disaster. But the iceberg had moved in too close, and the ship was about to crash.

The petite woman his sister followed scanned him from head to toe, then turned her attention to Nina. "Elise and I bumped into each other at the pasta bar. And almost literally." She laughed.

Nina did not. With Elise a few steps away, Nina flipped a hand in his direction. "Aretha, this is Greg Hernandez. Aretha is my roommate. And this is —"

"There you are," said Elise.

Greg glanced at Nina and saw her open her mouth to answer, when Elise added, "Have you seen Peyton? I thought he'd be with you." Elise peered over her brother's shoulders as if she'd spot her husband hiding behind him. And before he could reply, his sister looked at Nina. "I'm sorry. I must seem so rude. Aretha told me I had to see your dress. It's lovely, just as she said."

Elise placed her hand on Greg's shoulder. "I didn't know you knew my brother."

The words *my brother* hurtled into Nina and if she didn't soon salvage the emotional wreckage, she would be crushed beyond recognition. She willed herself into composure, clasped her hands in front of her to still their trembling. Standing between Greg and Aretha, she heard the gasp of one and sensed the flinch of the other. Nina had looked at neither one of the two as her mouth and lips formed syllables into words and pushed them out to answer Elise.

Nina's face paled and Greg winced when she said, "I didn't either."

Elise looked from her to Greg and back again, the question on her face unanswered.

"Excuse me, please. There's something I must attend to," Nina said and walked away from her boss, her friend, and her betrayer.

14

Somewhere between moving her arm out of reach of Greg's grasp, Aretha calling her name, and the ladies' room, which was her intended destination, Nina slammed into Brady Lambert. Make that Brady Lambert's camera lens.

She pressed her hands to her throbbing forehead, squeezed her eyes to ease the stinging, and hoped whatever she exclaimed at the moment of the crash didn't require a censor.

"Whoa! Ma'am, are you okay? I didn't see you . . . you walked by so fast."

She felt herself wobble, and Brady placed his hands on her shoulders. "I'm fine. I'm fine. I just need to sit down . . . some-where . . . ladies' room . . ." Something inside her welcomed the pain. It trumped the assault she felt her heart had just taken.

"Nina? Are we doing this camera collision again?" He sounded on the verge of annoyed, but Nina saw his expression soften when he looked at her. Brady cupped her head in his hands. "I'm so sorry. Here," he gently held her wrists, "let me see the damage."

If he could truly see the damage she felt, her body would be pumping fountains of blood. At least when he sees the tears in my eyes, he won't know they were already there. Nina slowly lifted her head as he moved her own hands away from her face. She hated and welcomed that his touch moved through her like a warm current. It had been a long time since he had held her so gently.

She sniffled and hoped her nose wouldn't be drippy as he brushed her bangs from her forehead, his fingertips whispers against her skin. Brady's eyes swept over her face, and she recognized that look of tenderness she knew he was capable of.

The orchestra broke into a medley of rock and roll tunes that sent couples around them scurrying to the dance floor. Pinched in the middle of the movement, he maneuvered them away from the swinging bodies to a bench along the ballroom wall. "The good news is you're not going to need to make an appointment with a plastic surgeon." He waited a beat, and when Nina managed a smile of sorts, he smiled, too.

126

"But," he said, and softly feathered her bangs over her forehead, "you're going to have a bruise the size of a tennis ball. I'd suggest not wearing your hair back for a while." He looked around and waved one of the servers over.

A barely-out-of-his-teens waiter walked over, his black bow tie slightly askew, balancing a silver tray ravaged by the hungry. "May I help you?"

"Yes, please," said Brady. "It seems my camera lens and her lovely forehead met one another on the dance floor, and it wasn't a pretty sight. Would you bring us some ice before it swells into an egg?"

"Do you need a doctor? We have an emergency . . ." His concern was tinged with a smattering of polite eagerness.

Sensing his anticipation of a reprieve from strolling through the guests, Nina was tempted to say yes to avoid disappointing him. But even if she did need medical attention, she wasn't going to subject herself to it here. The sooner she left, the better. "No doctor, but I appreciate your concern." Nina lifted her head to speak to him and the throbbing slipped into her temples. "Ice will be fine," she whispered.

The young man walked off, and Nina opened her purse in hopes of finding another tissue.

"Searching for one of these?" Brady handed her a handkerchief. "And don't look so surprised that I have such an old-fashioned item. These belonged to my father."

"I didn't mean to look surprised," Nina said defensively. "Just trying to keep my eyelashes from sticking together." She didn't, though, ever consider Brady a sentimentalist. Perhaps this was the new, improved version as designed by Janie. A woman who probably never had raccoon eyes. "I appreciate your help, but you don't need to babysit me. I can wait for the ice man," she said, swiping the handkerchief under her eyes as she spoke. "I'm sure you have other things to do."

"Babysit you? Did you really just say that?" Brady shook his head. "I know I didn't end our relationship with dignity. In fact, I should have apologized a long time ago for being so —"

"Arrogant?" Nina eyed him. Brady appeared as surprised to hear her comment as she was to say it. Maybe being honest resulted from a bashed head and not a broken heart.

He nodded. "I was going to say 'pompous jerk,' so you cut me some slack on that one."

He leaned against the wall, stared at the ceiling for a moment, then at the jitterbugging couples on the ballroom floor. "Sometimes, the grass is actually greener on the other side, but when you get there, you find out it's artificial turf. And you're wearing the wrong cleats."

In one of the full-length gilded mirrors in the ladies' room, Nina peered at the lump on her forehead It looked like a messy papier-mâché relief of Rhode Island. Brady had barely finished comparing Janie to fake grass when the server walked over with a small zippered plastic bag of ice. When she stood to leave, Brady told her he was going to take more shots of The AIDS Memorial quilt on display, but he'd meet her at the same spot in a few minutes. He insisted on taking her home. "It's a rule. When you hit someone in the head, you're obligated to drive them home." He had grinned, and Nina couldn't help but do the same.

She emptied the ice in the sink and tossed the bag away. No point now in freezing her forehead and having the condensation trickle down her face. Her pale cheeks, bare eyes, and washed-out lips provided little evidence of the time she invested hours ago applying her makeup. She started to reapply

129

her lipstick when her cell phone vibrated again in her purse. Talking to Brady earlier, she'd ignored the previous alerts. When she was ready to be found, like now, she'd let whoever might be looking for her know. Aretha had sent a text: "U OK? Where R U?????"

The multiple question marks loosely translated in Aretha-speak to, "I've been searching all over the place and can't find you and my patience is shot." Nina moved to the anteroom, found a bench to sit on, and started to return the message when the door slapped open and Aretha roared through.

"Finally!" Her friend's victorious tone echoed her hand pump. "You should be a magician . . . you've got that disappearing act mast— whoa, what happened to you?" Aretha grimaced as she pointed at Nina's forehead.

"Brady's camera and I had a bit of a collision." Nina touched the lump like it was a message written in Braille. Since it had stopped pulsating, it didn't feel as sensitive. But when she peered in the mirror, it didn't appear less angry.

"Was he trying to take a picture of you or something?" Aretha sat next to her, a shadow of suspicion on her face, and stared at Nina's forehead.

"Well, that would have been one heck of a close-up." Nina slipped her lipstick back into her clutch. "No," she said and paused to check her teeth, "in the heat of humiliation I wasn't paying attention to where I was going, and I walked right into his camera lens." When the door swept open again, Nina asked Aretha if Elise had followed her.

"I doubt it," she answered and waited until the young woman who entered walked past them. "I left your boss and her brother engaged in one of those 'who said what to whom and when' conversations. For what it's worth, he sounded intensely apologetic." She crossed her legs and bent over to adjust her sandals. "I know it's not my fault, but I'm the one who dragged Elise over there . . ."

"You're not the one who needs to apologize," Nina said. "I know I didn't flatter Elise when I talked about her. But did Greg have to humiliate me by being dishonest about himself? He knew Elise was already out of high school by the time I started. How was I supposed to make that connection?"

"Maybe I should back up before I say this," Aretha cautioned, "but 'didn't flatter'?

131

Really? Could that be a more textbook example of understatement? After Elise walked away, he told me about your conversation. How was he supposed to handle that? Would it have been less humiliating to be at the magazine talking about Greg to Elise, not knowing they were siblings? There was no way this was going to turn out well."

"Everything always turns out well for Greg Hernandez. The man leads a charmed life," said Nina, not even trying to mask the contempt in her voice. "And once again, I'm the one left to look like a fool."

15

"You're letting Brady take you home?"

"Don't make it sound like I'm riding with a serial killer," Nina countered while letting Aretha gently powder her forehead. "Do you want to come with us?"

Her friend moved her head from side to side to examine the coverage. "No, he's a serial dater. Isn't a whop on the head enough?" Aretha snapped her powder compact closed. "And, no again. I'm staying. I saw this beautiful man who is in one of my design classes, and he's not only dreamy, he's single. We took a taxi here, I can take one home."

"You're sighing, and that's a definite warning sign. Don't let your heart make promises your head can't keep," Nina warned as she and Aretha stood to leave the ladies' room.

Aretha opened the door and let Nina exit. "Sweetie, coming from you, that's a gem."

Had Brady not been waiting outside, Nina might have responded. But there he stood, looking more appealing than she wanted him to.

"Oh, hello Brady," said Aretha. She pointed at his camera. "Didn't they ask you to check your weapon at the door?"

"Aretha . . . ," he said and smiled, "you look stunning." Brady glanced toward Nina, then reached out and clasped Aretha's hand. "I've missed your wit. How are you?"

For a minute, Aretha's expression reminded her of Manny's slight head tilt when Nina used her nice voice to tell him how annoying he could be.

"I'm quite content, thank you. So, where's . . . um," Aretha paused, "Janie, yes, that's it. Is she here with you?" She smiled like someone who'd just trumped in bridge.

Nina opened her clutch to avoid eye contact with either one of them. She felt a bit guilty for enjoying Aretha's deliberate attempt to make Brady squirm. But, in typical Brady fashion, the master of finesse, he replied, "How kind of you to ask about her. She's still in New York." He looked at Nina. "At least the last time I spoke to her that's where she was."

Aretha replied, "I see," in a way that suggested she didn't at all. "So, I know you're providing transportation for the wounded." She nodded toward Nina. "Best of luck in the Big Apple." When she hugged Nina, she whispered, "Remember, it's just a ride home. And don't forget to take Manny out when you get there."

After Brady and Nina made their way around the dance floor to the front of the ballroom, he asked her to wait by the entrance while he had the valet bring his car.

"Can you hold on a few minutes? I wanted to bid on a quilt, and got distracted. I won't be long." The orchestra stopped as Nina opened the door to the ballroom and, of all people, Elise was on the stage announcing only five minutes remained for silent auction bidding. Nina watched as tables emptied, and people streamed into the quilt room, their voices swarming around them. She debated if she had the energy to swim along with the crowd, but remembering how perfect that quilt would be for Aretha, she decided to plunge forward.

"Nina, can I talk to you?" She felt the tap on her shoulder before she heard Greg's voice. And as much as she wanted to, there was no way to avoid him. But she could evade him, even if he had already moved

135

next to her. "Not now. I want to bid before the auction is over."

He stepped in front of her. "Please, this won't take long. I promise."

Not only did Nina not stop herself from rolling her eyes, she hoped her exaggerated display clearly conveyed her exasperation. They stepped to the side, away from the entrance to the room.

"Are you okay?" He stared at the lump on her forehead.

"Fine. I'm fine."

"Listen, I'm truly sorry —"

Nina held her hand up in front of his face. "Stop." She gripped her clutch with both hands. "Don't bother apologizing because, really, why should you now? You didn't all those years ago when you humiliated me. Why do you think it would matter to me now? At least, I know to not expect anything different from you."

Shoving his hands in his pockets, Greg stared at the floor. When he looked at Nina again, his face was taut. "I'm sure I deserve that. Tonight's not the time, but I can explain —"

"There's no explanation that can salvage the humiliation I felt all those years ago and what I felt tonight." Her head throbbed, but so did the buried resentment inside of her.

After so much time being held hostage in her heart, the words she wanted to say finally freed themselves. "You're right. Tonight's not the time. But there may never be another time for me to say I prayed that pain would bury itself in you like it did in me. After all, what would someone with money and popularity and success ever need to suffer through?" She noticed heads turning in their direction, and lowered her voice. "I used to feel guilty about that prayer, but after tonight, maybe not."

Something shifted in Greg then, and Nina sensed she'd driven the stake into his heart just like she'd intended. She could see his pride turn to ashes just as surely as if she'd set the fire. A momentary recoil, and he said, in a voice so severe she almost didn't recognize it as his. "You can stop praying now. Your wish has already been granted. And because of it, if not for God, I might not be here tonight to make you so miserable." He checked his cell phone that had pinged several times while he spoke. "I hope your night is better." He nodded and walked away.

His response was a hurricane force wind instead of the breeze she expected. And, had she not already been leaning against the wall, it might have brought her to the ground. Nina watched him, cell phone pressed to his ear, stride toward the stage as Elise announced that the auction had ended.

Brady waved at the valet when Nina met him again. "How did the bidding go?" His hand resting on her shoulder, he moved her toward the exit.

"Bidding?" *The quilt. You left to bid on the quilt.* "I don't know . . . I . . . I missed it."

Outside, the night air pushed against them like a damp sponge. Brady led her to a pearl white Mercedes so polished it could have been lifted from a velvet case. The valet opened the door, and Nina eased onto the soft leather seat and welcomed the cool air coming from the vents.

Brady adjusted his seat belt and, as the car pulled away from the hotel, he said, "So, what happened that you weren't able to bid?"

Nina stared out the window, still sifting through her emotional conversation with Greg. "One of the volunteers stopped to talk to me, and I didn't make it back," she said. That was all he needed to know, and it was enough of the truth to not make her uncomfortable manufacturing a story. Besides, it was his stories she was most interested in hearing. "Tell me about New York. It has to be more exciting than discussing quilts."

He turned down the volume on the Adele CD and drummed his thumbs on the steering wheel. "Maybe not more exciting." Brady stopped at the red light and looked at Nina. "I'm not as certain about moving as I was when Elise asked me to go. Especially because of Daisy."

Daisy? New York? This must be my night for sabotages. She knew she couldn't let being stunned betray her or else Brady might stop talking. As she opened her purse to shut her cell phone off, she said, "Yes, of course," as if she'd yawned the words out.

"When Janie first told me about Daisy, and everything going on with her family, it made sense that she'd want to live close. Then, Daisy started wavering about the decision. She didn't know what to tell Elise she wanted to do about the New York job after all she'd done to get it for her . . . I turn up there, right?" Brady pointed to the street ahead.

Nina nodded and hoped her composure would last longer than the rest of the drive.

"Anyway, now Janie's playing armchair therapist and big sister to Daisy, and she's neglecting everything else she needs to do to prepare herself for this new position."

"You mean neglecting you?"

Brady slowed the car as he turned into her driveway, then shifted into park. "Janie's helped me realize something," he said and looked at Nina.

She wanted to repeat her eye-roll performance, but his serious expression actually surprised her. Once again, she relied on her airy tone. "And what is that?"

"I know what it feels like to not be important in someone's life anymore, especially when that person is someone you thought wouldn't disappoint you." He cleared his throat. "I wasn't at all kind to you, Nina, and I hope you can forgive me for being such an idiot."

So, this is betrayer and forgiveness night? Whatever hope she felt by his admission was reined in by suspicion. *What was his agenda here?* "Forgive, yes. Forget, I'm still working on."

He leaned toward her, and Nina forced herself to ignore wanting to move closer and wait for him to kiss her. The space between them no longer felt like a force field, but a magnet. But she couldn't allow herself to be pulled in. At least not tonight. Brady moved his finger slowly down Nina's bare arm, from her shoulder to her wrist, then wrapped his hand around hers. "Maybe you won't have to forget. Forget what it was like for us to be together, I mean."

"I haven't forgotten what that was like, Brady." Nina slid her hand out from under his and opened the car door. "What I meant was I'm working on forgetting the damage you left behind. I'm not Plan B when you and Janie hit a speed bump on your way to wherever it is your relationship is going."

"You don't believe in second chances?"

Nina thought for a moment. "Brady, I don't even believe in first chances. People shouldn't take chances loving one another. Love should be intentional."

16

Greg was grateful for the text message that provided a legitimate excuse for him to leave Nina's presence. Her bitterness spewed from a wound that had festered so deep and for so long, that it had to be pierced to have any chance of healing. But her scathing attack and hearing that, for years, she wanted nothing more than for him to experience pain, horrified him. Would she be one of those people so full of hatred that, when it left, the shell she'd built to contain it would crack, and she'd find herself empty? Was this what happened to people who never knew or understood forgiveness? Who never asked, "Who were we to choose unforgiveness when God forgives us over and over and over?"

After Lily's death, he struggled desperately, knowing what he needed to do, but not wanting to do it. He wanted to feel anger, to build a shrine to it, and know that it would be there every day. Like Lily used to be. The accident, which he mostly didn't call it, as a man doesn't drink by accident or drive by accident, robbed him of his wife. It wasn't going to rob him of resentment and hate. Greg clothed himself in righteous indignation. But, with each passing day, the feelings weighed him down more and more until their weight almost broke him in two. Then he came across a quote from Corrie ten Boom, a Christian woman who'd been a prisoner in a Nazi concentration camp, "Forgiveness is to set a prisoner free, and to realize the prisoner was you." And that's when he had fallen on his knees and asked God to forgive his unforgiveness. Greg knew that only God working through him could make him strong enough to forgive the man who devastated his life.

But Nina didn't know or didn't choose to know that there was another way. Greg guessed she'd dragged the heaviness around so long, the thought of being weightless terrified her. Without the history, maybe the confusion about Elise would have been less traumatic for Nina. She probably thought he'd relay their conversation verbatim and, once again, she'd be the humiliated kid in the middle of the floor. Except this time it would be a ballroom floor.

As he told her she could stop praying for him to know pain, he saw glimpses of confusion in her eyes, as she scanned his face searching for evidence of dishonesty. Greg wanted to turn the wall behind them into a scoreboard, draw a line down the center, and ask her what she could write on her side that could possibly win out over his losing a wife and his daughter, a mother. But he wasn't going to use the memory of Lily as the highest score. Walking off when he did had spared each of them regret in the future.

The text, from one of the emergency clinics he'd recently worked in, updated him on the status of one of the sick animals he'd seen there. He went outside to call the vet tech who'd contacted him and saw Nina leave the hotel with someone driving a late model Mercedes convertible. She was going to miss the auction, which meant she wouldn't find out that he'd placed the highest bid on the quilt she wanted.

"Look, Manny, the princess is descending from her royal tower to join us." The dachshund yelped and trotted back and forth between Nina and Aretha, then sat to watch Nina walk down the stairs.

"Twenty years ago, I might have just stuck

144

my tongue out at you for that," said Nina, taking each step as if it were underwater.

Aretha grinned. "Twenty years ago, I might have followed that with running after your princess fanny." She pointed to the kitchen. "I made breakfast, but you missed the best part. Pancakes right off the griddle with strawberries and warm syrup. I saved a few slices of bacon, and you can pop the leftover cakes in the toaster or the microwave."

Nina sat on the bottom step and scratched Manny behind the ears as she listened to Aretha roll out the breakfast menu. "What time did you wake up to get all *Barefoot Contessa* on me? I couldn't have slept that late . . . did I?" Nina felt her wrist, no watch. She checked the pockets of her sleeping scrubs, no phone. "We need a clock."

"I've been saying that for months. It's after ten o'clock, so, yes, you did sleep that late. You left your cell phone down here, and your mother's been lighting it up like a Christmas tree with phone calls." Aretha yawned, and stretched out her arms and legs. "I woke up at the tender hour of eight o'clock. What time did you get to sleep?"

"You woke up at eight? I didn't go to sleep until after two, and you still weren't home. If you hadn't returned my text at almost one, I was about to put out a Missing Persons alert." She turned her phone off to avoid having to talk to her mother, zapped a cup of coffee in the microwave, and picked at the sliced strawberries she found in the refrigerator.

"Who knew Mr. Beautiful and I had so much to talk about? After we left the benefit, we drove around trying to find some place for breakfast. Ended up at Katz's Deli . . . had no idea how late it was until you sent that text." Aretha hugged her knees to her chest and smiled. "And why were you still awake? Having a long conversation with Brady?"

She decided to hold off telling her about talking to Greg before she left the benefit. Her emotional reserves were waning, and she had yet to deal with her mother. The Greg drama could wait, except for that last statement he made to her. The one about her prayer being answered already. It unsettled her, the way it did when she remarked one day that homeless people caused their own problems, and then found out Daisy had been one of those very people when her father left them.

Nina carried her coffee, a plate of bacon, and strawberries to the den, Manny following her waiting for crumbs to fall. "Sorry, buddy, you're out of luck today," she told him as she set everything on the coffee table. He resigned himself to curling around her feet. "For the record, my conversation with Brady ended not long after he turned into our driveway."

"Can't wait to hear this one."

Nina told Aretha the from-hotel-to-home story with Brady, hoping she sounded as lucid retelling it as she thought she was the night before. Since Aretha listened without an interruption, she must have achieved her goal.

"Have to admit, I wouldn't have thought you'd be able to stand up for yourself like you did. I suspect somewhere in that heart of yours there's a pitter-patter left for him."

Nina shrugged. "I suppose, but I wonder if I want a victory over Janie more than a relationship with Brady. Doesn't matter now. I don't have either one."

"Careful," warned Aretha. "You're back-sliding into your comfortable victim role." She checked her cell phone and smiled. "Mr. Beautiful just sent me a text. He wants to take Manny and me for a walk, and lunch." She patted Manny on the head. "We have a date. Aren't you excited?"

Manny blinked a few times, then he assumed his sleeping position.

"He's not understanding this concept of dating, since it doesn't happen too often around here. And, in case I'm here when he shows up, does Mr. Beautiful have a real name?"

"Luke. Luke Samuelson. And when I return, you're going to tell me why you were on sleep deprivation. But now I'm going to look for that cinnamon V-neck sweater of yours that I love to wear."

"It's either in the laundry room or my closet. Better hope it's in the closet . . ." Nina said. She wasn't sure she wanted to tell Aretha she stayed awake researching writing positions available in New York, places to live there, and more background information for her political corruption story. Then again, watching Aretha bounce down the stairs waving the sweater like a victory flag, Nina wasn't sure Aretha would care.

Nina mentally reviewed the excuses she could give her mother for backing out of lunch, but her mother would know that's exactly what they were. And she'd label them all flimsy and tell Nina any daughter who invented excuses not to have lunch with her parents probably didn't deserve them. She'd already called Nina six times in

148

three hours, so Nina's failure to return calls meant not only was she now up the proverbial river without a paddle, she just drilled a hole in her boat.

She counted to ten then forced herself to hit her parents' phone number. Less than three minutes later, it was all over. After Nina stumbled through the news she wouldn't be there, her mother responded with, "Good. I called so often this morning in an effort to inform you not to come here today because your father and I didn't feel up to company."

Was there any point in mentioning that someone's own daughter shouldn't be considered "company"? Except that in her parents' house, that's exactly how Nina felt. Apparently they did, too.

Nina checked the time on her phone. Unless she wanted to meet Mr. Luke the Beautiful in her wrinkled, hot pink, polka-dotted scrubs, she needed to find something more presentable to wear. A quick shower, a pair of jeans, and a black turtleneck later, Nina declared herself ready when the doorbell rang. She tapped on Aretha's door as she opened it. "He's here," she announced to an obviously undressed roommate who looked uncharacteristically frantic.

"I don't know what to wear." She sat on

her bed and held up a pair of black pants, "These make me look like I'm ready for Halloween wearing them with that sweater. And these," she tossed a pair of jeans to the floor in disgust, "are too tight. . . ."

The doorbell rang again. Aretha hissed, "Don't just stand there. Go let him in before he thinks no one is home."

Nina looked in Aretha's closet, shoved hangers back and forth, parting waves of clothes until she reached for a pair of khaki pants. "Here, wear these. They're capri length on me, so they should be the right length for you. And let it be known that I'm nice to you even when you're not." She heard an "I'm sorry" as she closed the bedroom door.

She scooted Manny out of the way, and opened the front door, anxious to see the man who captured her friend's attention. Instead, she saw the one who once captured her own.

Brady Lambert stood on her doorstep behind a bouquet of far too many long-stemmed white tulips.

"I wanted to surprise you," Brady said as he handed Nina an armful of flowers. "And make sure you didn't still have a lump on your forehead."

Nina held on to the tulips like she was hauling delicate firewood. "Well, you've surprised me," she said, still slightly stunned. "Um, thank you for these . . ."

"May I come in or were you on your way out?"

Dressed in his typical starched, button-down shirt and knife-pleated jeans, Brady always had that "on his way to somewhere" look. Unlike Nina who tended to look like she wasn't sure where she was going. Like today.

"Of course. I wasn't going anywhere," she said, but then wished she hadn't admitted it because she just lost an out for his leaving. She juggled the bouquet and tried to hold Manny back from dashing out the door as Brady entered.

"You're not Luke." An equally surprised, but finally dressed, Aretha peered over the steps after Nina shut the door.

"Hello again, Aretha. And, no, I'm not." Brady smiled, but not unlike someone who just told the cat where the canary was hiding. "Just checking on Nina's injury."

Nina set the tulips on the counter and moved her bangs aside to show Brady the swelling had gone down. "No more egg. Just a little bruise."

She found the only vase-like accommodation for such an armful of flowers, a tall ice bucket. She filled it with water, tried to arrange the not-so-cooperative tulips, and hoped Aretha would save her from a task at which she was totally inept. Nina watched her friend descend the stairs, and she wasn't rushing to help. In fact, she leaned against the granite bar, arms folded, and surveyed Brady and his flowers.

"Great choice, Brady," Aretha said. "Nina, I think you may have to trim the stems." She looked back at Brady. "Don't worry, that won't lessen their meaning."

Nina rifled through rubber bands, a collection of twist ties, and pens in what was supposed to be the utensil drawer for the kitchen shears. "Meaning? What meaning?" She found the shears mixed in with ladles and spatulas. "Aha," she said and held them up like a trophy. No one else seemed to be impressed. Not even Manny who growled as if on a timer, every few minutes, at nothing or no one in particular.

Brady cleared his throat. Without a camera slung over his shoulder, he lost his casual, cool factor. He looked so uncomfortable, Nina almost felt sorry for him. Almost. "The florist told me they mean, um, forgiveness. I guess since Aretha hinted at it, it must be true."

She looked from Brady to Aretha. "How did you know this?"

Aretha walked over and took the shears from Nina. "Because studying design isn't limited to furniture. I wouldn't want to decorate a lawyer's office with lavender, which signals distrust." She snipped the stems of the tulips and dropped them into the ice bucket. "Not the most elegant of containers, but the rustic look offsets the tulips quite nicely."

"She can't help it. The decorator gene just has to flaunt itself," Nina explained to Brady as she placed the arrangement in the center of the kitchen table.

Aretha tossed the pile of stems in the trash. "Okay, I'm done here. Going back upstairs for the finishing touches." She patted Brady on his arm. "Best of luck in New York," she said.

He opened his mouth as if he intended to respond, but instead he smiled and nodded. "Thanks, Aretha. I appreciate that."

Since Brady had never arrived unannounced, Nina wasn't sure of the next step. Or if he had one in mind. She wanted to stay and meet Luke, but the thought of four people as awkward as strangers in a crowded elevator nixed that idea. But close quarters in Brady's little convertible, when he looked and smelled so appealing, and her defenses were weak from the same environment less than twenty-four hours before? Another idea she should nix. But she had to do or say something to counteract the weird vibes.

"Would you like something to drink . . . coffee . . ." she opened the refrigerator, "diet drink, water . . . not much else there."

"No, thanks. I can't stay long, but I thought, maybe, we could talk," he said, glancing up the stairs.

Talk as in without Aretha overhearing. Okay. You're on.

"Sure. I need to take Manny out for his post-breakfast stroll. I'll leave a note for Aretha, and then we can go." Nina scribbled a smirk-inducing note, "Manny and I out with Brady. Please don't hate me for dognapping Luke's excuse for a walk. Back soon," and they headed out.

"There's a dog park about a block down on the right. He likes hanging out there," said Nina. Manny trotted ahead on the sidewalk, ears flapping. "Funny you should stop by today. Usually I have dinner with my parents on Sundays. If I hadn't over-slept, I would have really been surprised to find flowers on my doorstep."

"More surprised than you were to find me?"

"No, I suppose not. I don't remember you ever making unannounced visits . . ." Nina reined Manny in closer, and moved off the sidewalk when she saw a tricycle headed their way.

"Sadly, I don't think I did." He slowed his stride to match Nina's as Manny intermittently sniffed bushes and gardens along the way.

"You said you wanted to talk. About . . . ?"

"I heard you're going after that political corruption story. Impressive," he said, and he actually sounded as if he meant it. "You seemed out of your element at that society benefit."

Nina blinked a few times. She saw Brady, but her mother's voice just popped out of his mouth. "And that means, what exactly?"

"I meant that as a compliment. I think you have more to offer as a journalist than writing about the Houston movers and shakers and their charity galas. Daisy told Janie you drew the short straw on covering it because she wasn't there."

Apparently, he was researching last night as well, but his information source had to have been Janie, not Google. They reached the park, and Nina hooked Manny's leash to one of the stakes and let him roll and flop in the grass. She and Brady sat on a wrought iron bench facing a fountain that, depending on the breed, served as a watering hole, a swimming pool, or both.

"Was this what you wanted to discuss? My choice of assignments?" Nina brushed off her black sweater, which had become a haven for pollen, falling pine needles, and whatever other smut was in the air. Smoke drifted from across a wooden fence that bordered the park, and the unmistakable scent of barbeque must have reached her and Manny at the same time. They both turned toward the aroma, though Nina hoped she didn't sniff quite as noticeably as her dog did.

Brady crossed his leg over, resting the ankle of one leg on the knee of the other. He tugged a bit at the hem of his jeans. "I called Janie this morning, and I suggested she postpone the party she's been planning to celebrate the New York move."

"Postpone it until when?"

"Until I decide if that's really what I want to do."

17

Nina unhooked Manny's leash, freshened his water bowl, and read the note Aretha had left in place of hers. "Mr. B and I going out to eat . . . ."

She and Brady hadn't been gone that long, so Luke must have arrived right after they left. Nina wished she could text Aretha to relate yet another bizarre Brady-encounter. He'd left as soon as they returned, walked straight to his car, and said he'd be in touch. All Nina could think was, "Why?" Calling off Janie's party? The man must have a death wish. Or at least no fear of finding himself a mangled mess in an ER. But the man who recently growled at her after she saturated his expensive sweater with coffee was now purring?

If today and yesterday were math problems, the addition was definitely off. She wasn't sure what was missing from the equation, but her gut suspected an unknown variable. Her gut also rumbled its need for food, but nothing in the refrigerator looked as appealing as the barbecue over the park fence had smelled. She found the menu for Happy All Cafe and decided a delivery order of Beef with Orange Peel and Chili Peppers would silence her stomach.

While she waited, Nina opened her laptop to check the news. Brady's obvious admiration for her story flattered her, but his comments about her being at the benefit were flashbacks to his tendency toward elitism in journalism. For Brady, what you wrote reflected who you were and where you were on the magazine staff food chain. By trashing the fund-raiser, he unwittingly threw down the gauntlet. Proving Brady wrong might be worth investing herself in a feature story that didn't have the power to expose the corruption of local governments. After she finished her news story, she could elevate a feel-good feature into something that garnered attention.

She jotted some notes to check on Monday, then looked up The AIDS Memorial Quilt site. Aretha and her overnight infatuation arrived at the same time as her food. Manny almost collapsed from his barking frenzy after the delivery man and another strange male invaded his territory. Nina could hardly hear Aretha introduce this tall, ebony version of Patrick Stewart. He exuded charm, but not the kind that made Nina feel like she'd just been dipped in a vat of oil. He stood in the kitchen as if he'd been there all his life and watched Manny with calm amusement.

After several minutes of Manny's performance for Luke, which included a snarling rendition, Aretha grabbed his leash. "Come on, mister, we're going to take this Oscar-winning mad dog routine to the street," she said. He stopped barking, but locked his eyes on Luke while she attached the leash to his harness. Aretha handed Luke a dog biscuit, "Here, put this in your pocket. And if you value that strong hand of yours, don't put it anywhere near his mouth for now."

By the time they returned, Luke was Manny's new best friend, one worthy of lap jumping and face licking.

"The man must be a dog whisperer. I've never seen Manny fall so fast for someone," Aretha remarked

Nina smiled. Luke seemed to be an Aretha whisperer as well.

"If I can know I don't like somebody in less than two days, why is it impossible to know the reverse of that?" After dinner, Aretha stretched out on the sofa with her sketch book propped on her bent legs, moving her pencil back and forth between her palms as if she was rolling dough. "You think I'm crazy, don't you?"

"Yes, but I've always thought that." Nina looked up from her laptop where she sat at the kitchen table, half-hidden by the bucket of tulips. She bookmarked her page, then moved the flowers over so she could see Aretha. "You mean the Luke thing? For starters, you certainly weren't crazy about the beautiful part. That he is. If you tell me the two of you are running off to Vegas tomorrow, then you're definitely certifiable."

The pencil stopped. "Not tomorrow, of course not." It started again. "But I do like him. As in, if he doesn't call me this week, I'll be in mourning. And devastated. And maybe therapy." She started sketching again.

"Now that, my friend, is crazy. You met him less than two days ago. Have you even run a Google search on the man? Checked out one of those sexual predator sites? Due diligence. Do it."

Her pencil danced from one side of the pad to the other as she spoke. "Is that distrust because that journalistic blood of yours flows through the river of suspicion? If I told you he was an attorney or a doctor, you'd feel better?"

"Maybe, but being a doctor or lawyer doesn't save people from being skanky. His career choice isn't the issue."

"True, but would you even be the slightest bit interested in Brady if he worked as a mechanic or a plumber?"

Nina laughed. "Sister, I'd be more interested because I'm certain his income would be much better in those two careers. Why? Do you think I'm a job-snob?"

She shrugged. "Nah. You'd be more interested in Dr. Vet if you were, regardless of his sibling."

Nina pushed the flowers to the other end of the table. "Being a veterinarian doesn't exempt him from anything, and it's not his sibling who's an issue. Except that it's one more reason to distrust him. I know his history, and that's the reason I'm not interested."

Aretha looked up at Nina. "Kind of a shame, really. He is."

Nina lowered her Coke to the table. "He's what?"

"Attracted to you. I saw it at the benefit. His body language, the way his eyes lingered on your face —"

"Stop. Not only would he be wasting his time, just the thought of that makes me wish

161

I could give my brain a bath," Nina said.

"Okay, we'll go with that for now."

Nina considered raising another objection, but she didn't want another Greg conversation. And she knew Aretha had a way of drawing things out of her. Admitting she might have had just the flicker of a feeling for him wasn't news she wanted Aretha to use as evidence.

Manny pattered back and forth from the sofa to the table motored by a whine that grew louder with each trip.

Aretha, still focused on the pad, said, "He's hungry."

Nina had already headed for the dog food. "I'm on it." She spooned the canned duck formula into his bowl, and Manny tap-danced below her while she mashed it up for him. "Look," she said as she set his bowl on his doggy placemat, "I'm not telling you it's ridiculous to want to spend more time with Luke. I just don't want to see your picture on the television one night as a crime statistic." She washed her hands and sat down at the laptop again. "What does he do? And what are you so busy sketching over there?"

"He's a detective." She grinned as she turned the sketchpad to face Nina. The name *Luke,* styled in a fanciful calligraphy,

stretched from one end of the page to another.

Nina groaned. "Great. He brings out your
junior high tween-self."

18

Omitting the praise from Brady about her nose for news and his benefit bashing, Nina pitched the feature idea to Aretha. "I think writing human interest stories about the families in these support groups could earn me some promotion points, don't you?"

"That's your angle? Promotion points? Do you want to write these stories?" Aretha had retired her sketchpad for the night and folded towels fresh out of the dryer. The scent of Mountain Spring fabric softener competed with the lemon oil Nina was using to polish the table.

"Can't this be a case of the end justifies the means? I'm not all that excited about chummying up to these families, but if the end result is a ticket to New York, I could stand it."

"And you're not afraid that the stories will reflect your wafer-thin veneer of compassion? And you're comfortable using these people?"

Nina refolded the dust cloth and wiped the kitchen table again. "You're making me feel like a con artist. If their message gets out, will they care? Isn't that the Christian thing to do . . . you know . . . sacrifice for the greater good or glory or something like that?"

Aretha shook her head as if Nina had just said she'd eaten a bowl of jellybeans for breakfast. "A little advice. Don't go trying to be something you're not. Or, worse, be condescending because they operate on a level of faith."

"They'll be happy to have a forum to promote their cause. And I'll be happy to have a cause to promote myself. It's a win-win," Nina said.

Aretha moved a stack of dish towels into the kitchen drawer. "You better check your attitude at the door, that's all I'm saying."

Nina stayed awake long after Aretha had gone to bed. After Saturday night's identity confusion, Nina wasn't sure what the temperature of her boss's mood would be. She wanted to be ready for Elise in the morning, and that meant doing her homework that night.

What she discovered about The AIDS Memorial Quilt was more than she could digest in one late night–early morning research session. Knowing the weight (54 tons) and number of panels on the quilt (over 47,000) were almost trivial compared to its impact since 1985 when it was conceived. In 1987, a small group gathered in San Francisco to not only create a memorial for people who died of AIDS, but for that memorial to help everyone else understand the impact of the disease. A year later, the quilt had more than eight thousand panels. Eight years later, the quilt covered the entire National Mall in Washington, D.C. That would be the last display of the entire quilt because it became too heavy and too unwieldy to continue. Visitors to the quilt numbered more than eighteen million.

By 2008, the Memorial Quilt bore the names of more than ninety-one thousand men, women, and children who had died from AIDS. Since the inception of the Memorial Quilt, the tours raised more than four million dollars to heighten awareness of AIDS. The names on the quilt included babies who had died of AIDS from being breast-fed by their infected mothers, people who died from blood transfusions . . . the stories were endless.

Nina fell asleep scrolling through panel after panel after panel after panel.

■ ■ ■ ■

Driving to work the next morning, Nina pulled through the first Starbucks on her route, ordered an extra shot in her latte, and hoped she wouldn't nod off at a red light. She'd stayed up until almost three o'clock researching the We Care benefit and The AIDS Memorial Quilt, determined to show Aretha that the only story waiting to be found was a "feel good" feature that showcased the sewing talents of a team of little old lady quilters and the charitable contributions of the Houston wealthy.

The benefit had the potential to garner that promotion she wanted. Nina figured that if she could track down some families, she could expand one story into almost as many as Elise would give her space to feature. How tough would it be to pretend to be emotionally invested in their lives for a week or so?

All she needed was a buy-in from Elise, and Nina knew she could summon enough enthusiasm for the story just thinking about the pay-off. By the time she had parked her car, Nina knew the angle she'd pitch to Elise. And by the time she walked through the front door of *Trends*, Nina had practiced it enough that she felt confident she'd impress her boss.

"Good morning, Michelle." Nina tossed her empty coffee cup away and headed for her desk.

"Not so fast. The delivery service dropped this off for you," said the receptionist and handed Nina a box large enough for a winter coat. "It's kind of heavy. You might want to just open it here. Unless it's something private . . ."

"Michelle, for anything private to be this heavy, it would take half the shelves in Victoria's Secret." Nina set her purse on the counter. "There's no return address. You sure it's not going to explode?"

"I didn't hear any ticking, plus it came through the service we use all the time." Michelle handed her a pair of scissors. "I mean, anything's possible, but it just doesn't strike me as a bomb-like package. Especially because," she turned the box around where a piece of the brown paper had been torn, "I recognize this paisley wrapping paper." She spoke barely above a whisper, "It's cotton and silk. Ex-pen-sive."

Nina, joining the whisper conspiracy, said, "And how do you know it's so ex-pen-sive?"

"Because Elise asked me to order gift wrap from this company online, and I saw

168

it there. It's not the pattern she used, though."

"Interesting . . ." said Nina as she cut the brown paper away and revealed the teal and pink paisley patterns splashed against the white silk paper like peacocks. She and Michelle examined both sides of the box, but they didn't see a card. She carefully cut the wrapping paper away, and opened the box underneath. Taped to the tissue paper, its shades matching the paisley patterns wrapping, was a square white envelope.

Nina opened it, saw the initials at the top of the card, and quickly scanned the note. "You've got to be kidding."

"What? What does it say? Who's it from?"

She slipped it back into the envelope, which she knew would only increase Michelle's curiosity, but she didn't want the office involved.

If Nina hadn't opened the tissue paper when she did, Michelle was so impatient, that she might have done it for her.

Underneath the layers of tissue was the quilt she meant to bid on at the We Care benefit. The one she wanted to give Aretha for her birthday.

The monogram at the top of the note was the letter H between a G and an L. The note read, "Nina, I hope your friend cherishes

169

this quilt. I know, due to circumstances that night, you were unable to place your bid. It would have been a shame for your friend to miss your thoughtfulness. Regards, Greg."

"Don't you want to take it out?" Michelle ran her hand over the fabric.

"I know what it looks like. Can you hold on to the wrapping paper? I'm going to take this to my car." Whether she ultimately intended to keep the quilt or not, the more people who saw it and heard about the special delivery, the more complicated the story would become.

"But . . . but . . . I'd love to see it." Michelle watched as Nina wiggled the top of the box back, looking from Nina back to the quilt as if she'd just been shown dessert and told she had to go to bed without it. "This is perplexing, Nina. Why are you in such a hurry to whisk this away? Are you okay?"

Nina heard Michelle's tone shift into mother-mode. "I'm fine. Just fine. I just don't want to make a production out of this." Seeing the receptionist slink behind her desk and quietly roll the wrapping paper, she felt guilty for her abrasiveness. "I didn't mean to sound so rude. I'll explain, but just not now."

"No, really. You don't owe me an explanation. It's not my business, and I shouldn't have intruded." She flashed Nina her receptionist smile, the one that came with the job. "I'll put this." she said and waved the roll of wrapping paper like a baton, "on your desk as soon as I'm finished."

"Thanks, Michelle. Really." She hesitated. "I'm sorry. It's not your fault." *If Greg Hernandez would just stay out of my life, I wouldn't have reasons to be angry.*

19

Greg set the kitchen timer as he did every morning and every evening to remind himself, and now Paloma, to give his daughter her medicine. One of the biggest threats to HIV-positive children was becoming resistant to the drug therapy, and one of the ways to become resistant was not following a schedule for the doses. Jazarah's meds needed to be administered at the same time every day, and it was crucial that she not miss a dose.

He also set his and Paloma's cell phone alarms as backup, or in case, for any reason, they might not be home at the dosage time. Lily had joked that Greg would make a deal with the Emergency Broadcasting System if necessary. When the routine started, it was Lily who scheduled the times so that, years later, when their daughter started school, she'd take her meds before and after the school day. Everything involved with caring for Jazarah, what to do with the laundry if she should cut herself, preparing a portable first aid kit, had been orchestrated by Lily. And now that he was responsible without her, Greg said a prayer of gratitude every day for what his wife did to insure their daughter would have everything she needed.

"Daddy, tiss me, tiss me!" Jazarah bounced up and down on her toes, her arms outstretched. Greg picked her up and twirled her around, both of them making sputtering airplane engine noises. At close range, he detected apple juice fueled his daughter's plane, and some of it was now spotting his lab coat.

"Big smacky kiss for Dad," he said, and she obliged by planting her cupid lips on his as he brought her in for a floor landing.

And, as he did every morning, he didn't leave without the pat down to make sure he had his cell phone in one lab coat pocket, his wallet in one pants pocket, keys in the other, and his worn copy of *My Utmost for His Highest,* a devotional book by Oswald Chambers that belonged to his father. Some days Greg didn't have time to read; in fact, many days it wasn't until he arrived home in the evening that he did. He just liked carrying it with him. Knowing it was there seemed to ground him.

After making sure for the fifth time that Paloma had the name and phone number of the clinic where he'd be that day, he left. He had taped a note to his steering wheel to remind himself to call Elise on the way. His first call went right to her voicemail, but she called back before he'd even finished leaving her a message.

"Just hanging up with Peyton when you beeped in. You're starting early today. Where to?"

"Outside of Houston. A clinic in Cypress. First time there, so I wanted to give myself some extra time."

"Smart move. Have some good books on your iPod? Between the distance and the traffic, you might get in one or two today. People tell you Cypress is outside of Houston, but it's going to feel like you hit the outskirts of Austin. So don't panic, unless you find yourself actually in Austin . . ."

"Guess I should have packed two lunches. I'll call Paloma and warn her not to hold supper, bath, or bedtime."

"Do you need me to do that for you?"

"No. Wait. Okay I got it. I got it." Greg said as if speaking to someone who doubted his sincerity.

"Excuse me?"

"Sorry, the GPS chick thought I wasn't

changing lanes. Anyway, I don't need you to call the nanny, but I do have a favor to ask," Greg said as he focused on the exit signs that were like huge shiny green tabs on a wide concrete tablet.

"I'm almost to my office. Want me to call you back?"

"I'll talk fast because I need you to know this before you get there. And try not to ask too many questions. I'll explain when I have more time." He told her about the quilt delivery to Nina, but he didn't want Elise to mention it unless Nina did.

"And why did you feel compelled to purchase this and send it to her?"

Elise's voice put its mom-clothes on, but Greg understood that she didn't know about Nina losing out on the bidding process, which he then explained. "If she does bring up my name, which is highly unlikely after Saturday night, please don't say anything about Jazarah or Lily."

"Strange request. You don't want her to know you're a single father of an HIV-positive child from Ethiopia and your wife died in a car accident caused by a drunk driver? Any particular one or all of those?"

Listening to his sister roll out his life that way, it sounded like a script from a sappy daytime drama. *If only it had been. I could have rewritten the script.* "I'm not trying to keep any of that a secret. Don't be dishonest if she asks questions. Which I know you wouldn't be, which is precisely why I wanted to talk to you. I just have to work some things out, and I don't want her to make decisions based on pity."

"All of this from a misunderstanding at the benefit?"

"Unfortunately, no. It goes back a long way. But that's something I'll have to tell you later."

"How much later? Never mind. I just pulled into the garage. I'll text you as the day goes on. And Greg . . . I know you wouldn't ask all this if you didn't have good reason. I trust you."

"Thanks, Elise," he said, relieved that she would back him and that he spotted the exit for 290.

Now if he could just convince Nina to trust him.

When Nina walked back into the office after moving the quilt to her car, Michelle was on the phone. She looked up when Nina passed, nodded, but her smile looked like one she'd worn the night before and forgot to take off. If she'd been Michelle, she would have picked up the phone and pretended to be on a call just to avoid a conversation. It occurred to Nina that perhaps the reason she didn't trust other people or their feelings was her assumption they might be acting out of the same motives she would. And since, most of the time, her feelings were such a cosmic mess, she barely trusted them herself.

Nina might have pondered that longer if not for two distractions. An email from Elise asking to see her, and a message from Greg Hernandez. Was her morning starting with sibling rivalry or was this a cooperative attack? She needed a strategy and decided her best course of action was to see Elise first. If she spoke to Greg first, and the conversation crashed and burned, which she expected, then Greg might have time to relay that to his sister before Nina saw her. Then again, she had to ask herself if they would actually behave this way or was she, once again, presuming how they would act based on what she would do?

She had fifteen minutes before her appointment with Elise, so she opened her iPad and typed her pitch about the AIDS Quilt feature and facts about it that she thought would heighten its appeal. Nina checked the archives of *Trends* for any features similar to the one she wanted to write. With the exception of an article over seven years ago about an eighty-panel display at Rice University, there was nothing that would make the feature a recycle. She'd need a photographer, but Elise would have to make the call on that. No telling where Brady might be, especially in the next few weeks. He didn't seem to know where he'd be in the next few days.

Nina checked the time, examined the front of her black and white color-blocked dress for coffee spots, and applied sheer gloss to her lips. She looked over at Daisy's desk, and her stomach still hit her emotional bottom floor with an elevator-like thud. After hearing Brady talk about her being in New York with Janie, Nina suspected that thud might be permanent.

Before she saw Elise, she needed to find Shannon. She'd emailed the intern a list of questions, and she wanted to discuss the possibility of Shannon joining her on some of the interviews and possibly going to some of the quilter's meetings on her own. Nina walked around the office, but Shannon wasn't at her desk. She left a "please see me" sticky note on the intern's computer monitor, and entered a reminder in her iPad calendar to ask Shannon for her cell number.

Nina walked to the elevators, pressed the button, and almost went into cardiac arrest when someone suddenly came up behind her, squeezed her shoulders, and said, "Where do you think you're going?"

One yelp later, she whipped around to find Brady standing behind her.

"If you weren't so tall, and if I didn't value my iPad so much, I'd whack you on the head so hard, you'd be looking up at me when I was finished."

Brady laughed. "I wanted to surprise you. Obviously, I succeeded."

"That was not surprise you heard. That was fright. What are you now, twelve? Don't you know better than to sneak up on someone?" She pressed the button again and hoped he thought the warmth that she was sure flushed her skin signaled irritation not infatuation.

"I wasn't stalking you," he said and grinned.

The grin that, if Nina had been butter, would've melted her onto the floor. She stared at the doors to avoid eye contact.

"I just walked in, needed to go upstairs, and saw you waiting . . . it seemed amusing when I thought of it."

"Whatever. I think an alien child is overtaking your body." The elevator doors

179

yawned opened, and Nina stepped to the side to let Brady on first. No more blindsiding. "Why are you here anyway?"

"New dress? It fits you well."

Nina was relieved his eyes weren't hands. "Not new, and thank you. But you didn't answer my question about your reason for coming in today."

The door opened on Elise's floor and Brady exited with her. He pointed in the direction opposite from where she was going. "Human Resources. I have an appointment to discuss some matters there."

She didn't have time to ask for details, but she was beginning to realize the less she knew, the better. Brady seemed like a human boomerang lately. Every time she thought he'd be away for good, he returned.

"Good luck. I'm off to see the Dragon Lady."

She'd taken about four steps when Brady said, "Nina, wait."

Nina tapped her watch. "Can't be late. What's up and hurry?"

"How about dinner tonight?"

She thought about wanting to return that quilt to Greg. Or at least pay him for it. Nina considered the possibility of Brady being hungry for more than food, and the fact that she might welcome being on the menu.

She mentally duct-taped the voice of impulsiveness and answered, "I don't think tonight will work."

Disappointment replaced the invitation in his eyes. "No problem. I'll call later. You can tell me about your visit," he said, pointed in the direction of Elise's office, and walked down the hall.

Why would he think I'd be sharing information about an appointment with Elise? Brady acted as if his relationship with Janie was a wrinkle in time, and he'd simply stepped over it and back to her.

Those strange variables in the math equation that was Brady continued to increase.

20

Before Nina had an opportunity to dazzle Elise with her feature pitch, Elise announced that she officially released her from the bondage of human-interest stories.

"Daisy will be returning next week, and she can write the benefit follow-up." Elise scribbled something in her desk planner, and added, "When I talked to her this morning, she mentioned that it's the twenty-fifth anniversary of The AIDS Memorial Quilt, which would make a great sidebar story." She leaned back in her chair, tapped her pen against her hand, and stared out the window. "Probably a story all its own."

Anxiety fluttered over Nina like a sheet, and if she didn't move quickly, it would smother the very reason she wanted to see Elise. She clenched her iPad to avoid wringing the sweat out of her hands. She wanted to know why Daisy gave up New York or gave up on it, but that didn't matter now.

Nina sensed Elise's interest in this story and, if it was important to her, then it was important to Nina. "I have a better one," she blurted.

The pen stopped tapping, and Elise turned her chair to face Nina. "A better what?"

She flipped open her iPad. Seeing her notes settled her and sent the anxiety drifting to the floor. "A better idea for the benefit and AIDS Memorial Quilt. A feature series."

Elise leaned forward. "I thought you liked the hard-hitting, down-and-dirty news stories. This one could easily go to Daisy. I'm curious as to why you want it."

Nina knew the buy-in had to happen here, and it certainly couldn't be based on the means to the end pitch she gave Aretha. She had to convince Elise she had a stake in the story.

"Not everyone in Houston could attend the benefit, but we could bring the benefit to them. The story isn't the gala or even the Memorial Quilt itself because it's been around for a quarter of a century. The people are the story. The people behind all those quilts hanging on the walls that night. Every one of those quilts is a story, just like every panel of the Memorial Quilt represents someone. When we give AIDS a face, or in this case, *faces,* then contributing to or participating in the benefit isn't just about the quilts people can buy there. It's about the power of support and community giving people a way to work through their grief to create something of beauty that can honor those they love." Nina stopped because, though Elise nodded as she spoke and seemed focused, there would be no point in explaining more if she didn't approve.

"That's quite a passionate pitch. So, how would you make that happen?"

"My idea is to attend the support group meetings, follow a quilt from its inception to the final stitch. A different person in the group would be highlighted in each feature, with their permission, of course. The last feature would highlight The AIDS Memorial Quilt. We could go to D.C., and maybe some of the quilters could make the trip as well. In fact, with each story we could include the directions for making a panel and invite our readers to participate. They could form their own groups or just send the panels to us, and we could deliver them to Washington."

Elise walked over to the window of her office.

Nina waited. The quiet clanged in her head, but she knew if she didn't outwait Elise, she'd start babbling. She didn't want to beg for the story. Though she would if it came to that. She occupied herself counting the number of roses in the vase on Elise's desk, the number of pictures on the shelf to the right of her desk, and she was about to start counting the books when Elise broke the silence.

Still standing with her back to Nina, looking out the window, she said, "And you're sure you can do this?"

Inside herself, Nina jumped up and clapped. The outside Nina, firmly and clearly responded. "Yes, Elise. I can do this."

"Okay, then," said Elise as she returned to her desk. "Let's talk about the publication schedule, and we'll take it from there."

Almost two hours later, Nina didn't see any signs of Brady when she left Elise's office. She had a text message from Shannon asking if they could meet in the morning, and one from Aretha that she was meeting Luke for dinner. Three consecutive days? Did he not have enough detective work to keep himself busy? Maybe she should have accepted that invitation from Brady because it was about to turn into a drive-through fast food or pizza delivery night. She scrolled through her messages and saw a few numbers she didn't recognize that she'd have to check against her contact list that could be callbacks for her political story.

She opened her iPad and glanced at the pitch she had prepared for Elise. With the exception of the first sentence, nothing she said to Elise came from the original pitch she'd written. Looking at those words now, they seemed hollow, commercial. How did she manage to summon such passion for this feature? Wherever it came from, it rang true enough to Elise. And that was enough for Nina.

It wasn't until Nina opened her car door that afternoon and saw the large box on her back seat that she remembered the day had started with the quilt delivery from Greg Hernandez.

Her original knee-jerk reaction plan — to find out where Greg lived, then march to his door with all the righteous indignation she could gather and her checkbook, demand that he either take it back or take a check in payment — required revisiting. Telling the brother of your editor that you refused to keep the very item you used as the centerpiece of your pitch was likely a prelude to her assigning you obituaries and

186

weddings.

Still, she didn't feel comfortable giving Aretha a gift that she didn't buy, and it would be dishonest of her to not tell her it came from Greg. So, she needed to figure out a way to contact him without involving Elise because that would take uncomfortable to an entirely new level. She could explain why she wanted to reimburse him, and if he wouldn't tell her what he paid for it, there might be a way for her to contact the benefit organizers. *Really, Nina, what kind of journalist are you if you can't get someone's address or find out what that quilt sold for?*

Her rumbling stomach interrupted her. She'd been occupied with scenarios in her head and neglected the ones involving food. At the traffic light, she called Aretha thinking they might not mind if she joined them. Brazen, but how intimate does dinner have to be when they'd just started dating? When Aretha answered, she told Nina they wouldn't have minded at all except they were already on their way to Kemah.

"You're driving almost an hour across Houston to Galveston Bay for dinner?"

"It's not that far." She stopped to tell Luke who she was talking to. "We felt like eating seafood, and the weather's so nice, we thought when we got to Kemah, we'd spend some time on the Boardwalk."

"Okay, then. I'll go to Plan B."

"Sorry. If you get desperate, there's still a pizza in the freezer." *I'm becoming Plan B.* Nina heard the distraction in her voice. She imagined Aretha talking to her while she pointed out places to Luke along the way or that shrug and partial eye-roll while she mouthed, "Sorry . . . won't be long" to him. "That would be Plan W. I'll figure something out. See you later."

A few blocks away from home, she pulled over for gas, and considered calling Brady. But he told her when they were both outside Elise's office that he'd call her. Making the first move toward anything resembling a date could send the wrong message to Brady. A small voice within her tapped on the shoulder of her conscience and whispered, "But what if it's the right message?" She hushed it as she settled in her seat and closed the car door. "Guess we'll both have to live with no message," she said to the steering wheel and started the drive home.

At least she knew one male who'd be excited to see her. Nina just wished he didn't have four legs and a cold nose.

After gaining no satisfaction from a round of sniffing to determine if the large box

Nina set on the coffee table was edible and paw slapping it to elicit a squeak, Manny ignored it and returned to his rawhide bone.

"Well, since Aretha abandoned us both, at least I can look at this without having to sneak around, right?" Manny didn't even bother to stop chewing. "You're going to have to be better company than that if we're going to be spending more time alone, mister."

She opened the box, carefully lifted the quilt, and spread it out on the sofa. Removed from the other quilts on display that night, its explosion of color and sophisticated, bold design were more evident. And made it all the more perfect a gift for her friend. On one corner, an attached, hand-stamped card read. on one side: Threads of HOPE, stitched by people of FAITH, for those we LOVE. On the other was a thank-you for purchasing the quilt and a telephone number. A label sewn on another corner simply had the words: Threads of Hope, Jeremiah 29:11.

Nina entered the number in her phone and set a reminder to herself to call it in the morning. If she asked the cost of making one like it, she'd have an idea of what to offer Greg. And then, pulling a Brady, she could show up unannounced and drop it off. If she called him, he'd probably tell her he didn't want the money.

She placed the quilt back in the box then shoved it under her bed where Aretha would be least likely to look. Or vacuum.

By nine o'clock, Brady hadn't called, texted, or attempted any other form of communication. Nina surprised herself by not being surprised. Not following through was behavior more typical of the Brady she knew.

Now that Elise had assigned her the feature, Nina dragged out her laptop to continue researching. Manny, seeing her stretched out on the sofa, jumped up and wiggled next to her, resting his head on her knee. She started with the history of The AIDS Memorial Quilt, which went back to 1985, when the idea of the quilt sprang from the way placards of those who died with AIDS were placed against the wall of the San Francisco Federal Building. The first quilt, created in June of 1987, was displayed on the National Mall in October of the same year.

Nina thought about that first small group that met in a San Francisco storefront, afraid the names of those they loved would be lost forever, and so they created a quilt as a way to document their lives. Twenty-five years later, groups like the ones whose quilts were auctioned at the benefit, met to carry on that mission, to memorialize those who died of AIDS. Except that, and sadly, over the years, the names of women and children were added. From 1985 until the year 2000, the number of AIDS-related deaths in a year increased by 429 percent. Little wonder, with those statistics, why the quilt weighed fifty-four tons today.

Hours later, Nina still hadn't arrived at the end of her research, and Aretha still hadn't arrived home.

21

Greg checked his cell phone again. Nothing from Elise. By late afternoon, when Greg still hadn't received any messages or phone calls, he wondered if the quilt had even been delivered.

He contacted the delivery service and was told the package had been signed for early that morning. Two patients later, he sent Elise a text. Maybe Nina wasn't at work, so there wasn't any reason for Elise to contact him. Four patients later, she sent a text in response: "Nina here. No mention. Call me on your way home."

No mention of the quilt? The Saturday night episode? Both? Maybe he attached more importance to both than did Nina. Bypassing the drama was a relief, but bypassing any mention of having received the quilt seemed, well, like bad manners. And he'd already dealt with his quota of the discourteous by the time the clinic closed.

Like the couple whose Lab used the waiting room as his bathroom, then expected the desk staff to do potty patrol. And the little boy about his daughter's age who entertained himself rearranging the food and supplies merchandise on display while his father lifted his head from his e-reader every few minutes and said, "Stop that." He closed his car door, leaned his head against the steering wheel, and said a prayer of gratitude for his family. Compared to that gift from God, what did his receiving or not receiving a thank-you note matter?

Seeing the gridlock on Highway 290, Greg contemplated abandoning his car and walking the forty or so miles home. He should have brought along *Anna Karenina,* the 976-page novel Lily always wanted him to read. With this traffic, he'd stand a good chance of getting halfway through it. He still needed to call Elise, but he called home first. He talked to Paloma and affirmed that he wouldn't make it there until after Jazarah's bedtime. He could barely hear her for his daughter's chanting in the background. "Talk to Daddy. Talk to Daddy." Paloma excused herself, and Greg heard her calm, soft voice, "We must wait and be kind, and not speak when someone else is speaking."

When she returned, Greg expressed his

appreciation for her making sure Jazarah wouldn't grow up to be what Elise labeled an "S.B.K.," spoiled brat kid.

"You are welcome. It is my opinion that the two of you together in public will attract attention even if both of you say nothing. Her behavior will be scrutinized more so than other children's. This, I know."

And that was another reason she made the perfect nanny for his daughter. Like Jazarah, she, too, was adopted from Africa, an HIV-positive preteen, into a blue-eyed, blonde-haired, and freckle-skinned family. The attention was sometimes cruel, but Paloma learned grace and, as she said, "to stand on God's promises."

"One message before you speak to your sweet daughter. A lady, Amelia, called to say she and her husband will be in Houston next month, and they would like to visit. Now, here is Jazarah."

Amelia and Dale were traveling here? Thinking of them brightened his otherwise gray day. A train of questions rumbled through his head, but his daughter's lyrical chatter ran them off the track. Greg inserted a few "Really?" and "That's great" responses as she recalled what sounded like her itinerary for the day. Then, in the middle of a discussion of flowers and peanut butter, she announced, "Bye, Daddy!" and the conversation ended. He smiled imagining that Paloma setting the table for dinner diverted her attention.

His conversation with his sister didn't require many more responses than those he'd just used with his daughter. On her way home herself, Elise said she only had time to hit the highlights. Essentially, Nina pitched a feature series around the AIDS quilt and the local benefit that excited Elise. Their time together was focused on those details, so his name or Saturday night never came up.

"I have to say, Nina's passion for this project was unexpected. I called her in to tell her she was off the human-interest story hook, but she didn't want to let it go," said Elise.

"Yes, that surprises me, too," Greg said, too late realizing he just played a card his sister didn't know he held. He could picture her narrowed eyes as her brain whirled around what he'd said.

"Why would it surprise you?" The emphasis in her question fell on *you.*

How was he going to extricate himself from this one without revealing his conversation with Nina that night at the benefit before Elise arrived on the scene? He didn't want to tell her Nina complained about having to write a feature story and cooperated only because his dragon lady sister of a boss wanted her to. Something must have changed for her between then and today, and the last thing he wanted to do was something that would, once again, sabotage Nina. But, he couldn't lie to her either. *Good thing traffic's moving three miles an hour or I'd be too distracted to think.*

"When we first started talking, I didn't even know she was on the *Trends* staff. She mentioned how much she enjoyed hard-hitting news stories," he shared with Elise.

But Greg continued to wonder, for most of his journey home, what caused such a radical change of heart in Nina.

When Nina left for work, a fully-dressed Aretha was snoring, curled up on the sofa, the dog wrapped around her bare feet. Nina had finally dragged herself upstairs not long after midnight, so Aretha didn't make it back until after that. She checked Aretha's work schedule that she always left on the refrigerator to make sure she'd be safe not waking her up. She was off, and she didn't have any classes, so Nina skipped making breakfast and eased herself out as quietly as possible.

Michelle hadn't arrived yet, so Nina left the blueberry scone she'd bought for her on her desk. She wrote, "to M, from N, and I'm still sorry."

Shannon was already hovering around Nina's desk. "Do you need some help?" She looked like she wasn't sure what to grab first.

Her coffee in one hand, her oatmeal in the other, her purse, her iPad case, and her messenger bag slung over her shoulders, Nina perpetually had that pack-mule look about her. "Believe it or not, everything balances, so if you take just one item, I might topple over." She looked at Shannon as she placed her breakfast on her desk. "Did you eat? Need to get coffee or anything before we talk?"

"No, I'm good. I ate at home and brought coffee," she pointed to the petite stainless steel Thermos on her desk.

Nina peeled off her bags. "Another good reason to have your cell number. Next time I can call you on the way in." She sat down, stirred her oatmeal, and told Shannon to pull up a chair. "Since you're good to go, let's get started."

For the next half hour, Nina outlined how the intern could help her. "I'm sending you copies of what I've already put together for my story on the political corruption. I need you to fact-check and proofread what I have so far. Then, you'll need to open a file on your laptop, just label it 'Quilts' for now. And here's the information I want you to research." She handed Shannon a list starting with the We Care benefit, the sponsors, the contributors, background on The AIDS Memorial Quilt, local support chapters. Nina stopped there. She recognized the eye-darting, first-rung on the panic ladder look on Shannon's face. "If you have questions, ask me. Seriously. We don't want to have a problem with sources or research that might have been easily solved, okay?"

"Yes. Absolutely." Shannon stood up, and Nina imagined she felt the anxiety fall off like scales. "I'll get right on it."

Nina watched her walk away, but instead of going to her desk, she headed for the door. "Are you leaving?" She couldn't have overwhelmed her already.

"Just long enough to go to Brew Who next door."

"The coffee shop? But didn't you say you brought it from home?"

"Oh, I'm not going for coffee. I left my Bible there. A few of us have a short Bible study one morning every week."

Well, this piece of news went right over my

head. A Bible study? Seriously? "How did I miss that? You'd think for a place that reported news —"

Shannon looked like someone next in line to walk over hot coals. "We just started a few weeks ago. I mean, a few of us go to the same church. With the others, it was just word-of-mouth, you know . . . You're welcome to join us. Really. We never meant to exclude anyone . . ."

Nina flashbacked to a middle school moment, sitting cross-legged on the cold hard floor of the hallway on Valentine's Day, pretending to do homework she'd actually finished the night before. While girl groups giggled around her and exchanged hand-drawn cards, glittery red boxes of candy, and white fluffy stuffed bears whose hearts beat outside their bodies, Nina invested herself in the algebraic importance of helping *x* find *y*. Because none of the girls looked for Nina.

"Would you like to go with me?"

Shannon's question pulled Nina back to reality, but to one that didn't feel all that different than the one she'd just left. *But this wasn't one day of "will u b mine" messages. This was a lifetime of it. You don't even go to church. Or pray. Why would you want to go to a Bible study?*

"Thanks for the invitation. Maybe another morning, but tell me," Nina ate a spoonful of oatmeal. "Who else is there?"

Shannon started rattling off names, but it wasn't until Nina heard "Michelle, Elise . . ." that she had a coughing spasm from almost swallowing her coffee into her lungs.

Nina's fingers hit the telephone number for Threads of Hope, but her brain burbled at jet speed, ready to make a landing right into Aretha's ears. Even as she heard the phone ringing, the words "Bible study" stayed in her head like uninvited guests, the overnight variety.

She heard "Hello," on the other end. Finally, her mouth had something to do. Nina identified herself as a staff writer at *Trends,* forcing the belligerent child in her head to not blurt, "Who recently discovered she was ostracized from the Bible study." She informed the voice that she attended the We Care benefit, where she bid on one of their quilts —

"Which one?"

Nina told her it was the paisley-patterned quilt, which elicited a squeal. *How old are these people? This may be a more painful feature than I thought.*

"That's the one I helped sew. We really appreciate your support —"

This conversation may last longer than an all-day sucker. "I'm sorry what did you say your name was?"

She laughed. "You hadn't asked my name, but it's Crystal. My mother, Kelley, usually takes the calls, but she's out right now. Do you want her to call you back?"

Nina's tolerance groaned. "No, in fact, I think you can help me. I'd like to come to one of your meetings. The magazine would like to run a feature . . . but I can explain that when we see one another. When will you all be getting together again?"

"This Sunday at two o'clock. We meet at the Faith Church Fellowship Hall. Do you need directions? It's that little church —"

"I'm sure I'll be able to find it." *Otherwise, my GPS is worthless.* "Sunday at two, right?"

Crystal confirmed and when Nina hit "off" on her phone, she wondered how she was going to be able to pull this off.

22

"It's not that funny." Nina went downstairs to the lobby atrium where she called Aretha after hanging up with Crystal. The more she talked, the more Aretha laughed.

"Do you hear yourself?"

"Yes, and I hear Manny barking. What's your point?" Nina paced in front of a metal sculpture that looked as if someone had thrown car parts in a blender, then dumped them on the ground.

"Manny and I are stretching our legs. You, on the other hand, aren't stretching something enough. Sister, you're making that group sound like terrorists. Afraid they're going to sneak in the office and whomp you with their Bibles?"

"Don't be ridiculous. I don't so much care that they're having a Bible study. Though it does reek of 'look how holy we are.' I couldn't care less if they gathered to study the fax machine instruction book. What bothers me —"

"What bothers you, way down deep, is that no one included you. What bothers me is, why do you care? You don't go to church, you don't read the Bible . . . It would be like my getting offended because I wasn't invited to join the Garden Club. What do I know about gardens? I know things grow in dirt, and some are trees and some are flowers and then there's everything else."

"What does that say about what they think of me . . . that they didn't even think of me? I'm a good person." She located a padded bench next to a fountain wall. Nina considered pulling off her shoes and soaking her feet in the water.

"I'm guessing they think you wouldn't be interested. Being good isn't an admission ticket. And if you did study the Bible, you'd know that's something to be grateful for."

"If I'd known Elise was there, I would have been interested."

"Nina, are you really thinking you could use Bible study to earn points with your editor? I guess people fake it, but I don't see how they do. That's not a risk I'd be willing to take. Eventually, you'd be as obvious as a cat at a dog fight."

"Here's the thing . . ."

"Wait. Let me get Manny. He thinks he's

going to tear after Mr. Pete's Lab."

Nina examined her cuticles, not remembering the last time she and Aretha had a mani/pedi day. Maybe this Saturday. *What was taking so long?* She checked her watch. Time for her to get back to the office. She could finish talking to Aretha later. "Aretha, you there?" Nina tried again, louder, "A-retha . . ."

When she did hear her friend, her scream shot Nina up from the bench as if it had reached out of the phone and pulled her by the hair. Aretha shouted Manny's name, but Nina didn't hear him. "What's going on? Aretha? Where are you?" The pitch in her voice rose, and the words wrapped inside her so tightly she could barely breathe.

"Nina, Nina." Aretha sounded as if she'd just finished a marathon, but there was no mistaking the hysterical urgency.

Before she even heard the words that a car hit Manny, Nina had kicked off her shoes and sprinted up the stairs to Elise's office. With every step, she repeated, "Be there, be there, be there . . ." until her own breathing was as labored as her friend's. Nina had pushed on the phone speaker and when she started the stairs for Elise's floor, Aretha said, "Mr. Pete's helping. He's breathing, Nina. We'll take him to Dr. Alvarez —"

"No. Wait one minute. Just one minute."

She opened the stairwell door. Elise was standing outside her office on her cell phone. Nina saw what she felt mirrored in Elise's face.

"Nina? What happened?"

"Where's Greg? Please call Greg. Manny. Aretha called and said a car hit Manny." Nina didn't remember Elise's office being so cold. Her cell phone shook in her hands.

"I just hung up with him." Elise pressed call. "I'll call him back right now."

Greg must have answered because Nina watched Elise's lips move, but the words bounced like beads off a broken necklace.

"Is that your friend on the phone?"

Nina looked down at her hand and nodded.

"Hand me your cell phone, so I can tell her what to do." Elise said more words into the phone, then turned to her receptionist. "Would you cancel my lunch appointment? I'll be back as soon as possible." She handed Nina her phone, and closed her fingers around it. "Hold on to this."

"Greg?"

"He's going to meet us at the Animal Emergency Clinic. And I'm driving you there." She looked at Nina's feet. "You probably want to put your shoes back on. We're taking the elevator."

Greg, Paloma, and Jazarah were on their way to lunch, singing, "Don't worry about a thing, cause every little thing gonna be all right" along with Bob Marley when Elise called. As soon as Greg heard the sound of his sister's voice on the phone, he pulled into the first parking lot he could find. He sensed it wouldn't be good news.

"Hey, a car hit Nina's dog. She's here at work, and the dog was with Aretha, her friend. I know you're off today, but can you help? She asked me to call you."

"Shh! A few minutes for Daddy, okay?" Greg lowered the volume, and he needed only to exchange one glance with Paloma for her to distract his daughter with her new book, *The Very Hungry Caterpillar.* "I'll call Dr. Cadoree at the emergency clinic. I've done some relief work for him, so they can meet me there. Does Nina know anything about the dog's condition?"

"Doubt it, and if she did, I don't think you'd get too much right now. She's holding her cell phone, so Aretha might be on the line."

"Find out. I need to talk to her as soon as

I can. Time is crucial here."

Elise took Nina's phone and relayed information from one to the other. "Dachshund. Almost two. Neighborhood street, not going above 20. Breathing. Trying to move a bit. No blood in ears."

"Tell her to support his back, neck, and limbs and as gently as possible, wrap him in a blanket and head to the clinic. If someone can drive her, that's better, and please drive the speed limit. We don't want to have a dog hit by a car in the car with two humans who are hit by one."

Greg called the emergency clinic to tell them about Manny in case they arrived before he did. He didn't have time to take Jazarah and Paloma home, so they'd have to come with him. He figured Paloma, listening to the conversation, already understood the Elvis Presley Memorial Combo at Chuy's Restaurant wasn't going to happen. "Okay, Princess Jazarah, Daddy has to hurry to take care of somebody's little dog that just got hurt. So, you and Paloma will have lunch, then pick up Daddy, and we'll all go somewhere for ice cream."

"Um," she looked back and forth between Greg and Paloma. "Choc-lit?"

Greg smiled. "Of course. Whatever flavor you want. Do you want to sing some more?"

She clapped and kicked her feet against the bottom of the car seat. "Yes! Yes!"

When they pulled up to the clinic entrance, Paloma replaced Greg behind the driver's seat. "Here's my credit card. Call me when you finish lunch, and I'll let you know how I'm running on time." He opened the door and leaned in to kiss Jazarah. "Love you. Be good."

When Aretha arrived ten minutes later, Greg was encouraged Manny made it to the hospital. Animals that did, especially small ones, had a good chance of survival. And, if the car that hit him wasn't going fast, possibly a better chance.

23

Alone with Elise, no distractions, with time to discuss her future at the magazine, to solve the mystery of Daisy, Brady, and Janie . . . but, instead, Nina stared out the window and wished the car could move as fast as her heart pounded. The thought of what Manny might look like when they arrived at the emergency clinic scared her almost as much as the thought that she might not make it there in time.

Elise's phone rang, and she quickly muted the Bluetooth and picked it up off her seat. Nina held her breath and waited. As soon as Elise said, "Great," she stopped clutching the arm rest and came up for air. A few one- or two-word replies, then Elise hung up. "That was Greg. He said Aretha just arrived with Manny. When we get there, which should be in a few minutes, he might be in surgery. He said the fact Manny made it to the clinic is a really good sign."

When Elise pulled up in front of the clinic, she handed Nina the box of facial tissues from the back seat. "Take this. Do you want me to stay, because I can?"

"I'll be okay. Aretha's here. Thank you so much for . . . for everything. Calling Greg, driving . . ."

"I'm glad I could help." Elise squeezed her hand. "It's hard when someone you care about is hurt. But, look, Greg is a good doctor. Actually, he's a great doctor, and he'll do everything he can. And I'll pray for all of you."

Nina flashbacked to that morning, and her irritation over Elise and the others at Bible study. And now, she appreciated that Elise prayed.

"That means a lot to me. Thank you." Nina closed the car door, and she walked into the clinic. Aretha was at the counter filling out papers on a clipboard, and as soon as she saw Nina, she dropped the pen and hugged her.

"I'm so sorry, Nina. So sorry. Please forgive me." She sobbed, and Nina held her and patted her back.

"It's not your fault. You adore Manny. I don't blame you." Nina let the tears course down her cheeks for the first time since she heard Aretha's strangled voice telling her what happened. "Where's Mr. Pete? I was so confused when you called. How did Manny get loose? What happened?"

Aretha explained how she attached his leash to his collar because he wasn't wearing his harness. When he saw the Lab, he wiggled himself right out of the collar. "We were already on the sidewalk, so he didn't have far to go to get to the street. So, I'm calling him, and he stops. When I got closer, he took off." She paused, her shoulders slumped. "I didn't see the car coming, but the driver had to know he hit Manny."

"What do you mean, 'had to know'?"

"He stopped for a minute, and he looked at me, so I know he saw me screaming. Then, he took off."

Nina waved her hand in front of Aretha. "Wait. Wait. Wait. He did what?"

"He left. But," she pulled her cell phone out of her pants pocket, "not before Mr. Pete got a picture of his license plate." She scrolled through her pictures. "And he sent it to me, and I sent it to Luke." She showed it to Nina. "And whoever this is, will be getting a visit, I hope real soon, from one not-so-happy detective."

Nina finished filling out the papers and handed the board back to the receptionist.

"Thank you," she looked at the top page, "Miss O'Malley. My name is Tessa. Dr. Hernandez will be out to talk to you as soon as he can. There's a little kitchen area down the hall," she said and pointed to a door on her left, "if you want something to drink, and there's a machine with snacks." She smiled and added, "Some of them are even healthy."

"Do you know how much longer he'll be?"

"No, I don't. But, since you're the only ones here right now, I can go back and check for you."

Nina sat next to Aretha who already had a little pile of crumpled used tissues in her lap. "I'm so glad Elise gave you these. I've been wiping my face and my nose on my T-shirt."

Nina looked at her herringbone cropped jacket and trousers, her black silk shell. "Manny's worth a dry cleaning bill, right? Not like he hasn't cost either one of us that before."

"Miss O'Malley," Tessa held a door open off the waiting room, "Dr. Hernandez said you can see Manny now."

Nina and Aretha walked into the treatment area where Greg and a young man in scrubs hovered over Manny.

Nina felt her heart pinch. "He's okay,

212

right? I mean, he's so still . . ."

"We gave him something to tranquilize him," said Greg as he waved them closer to the table and moved aside so Nina could stand near Manny.

As if testing the temperature for one of Manny's baths, Nina reached out until her hand rested on Manny's soft, warm fur.

Greg told Nina. "You have a few options, though I'm sure you won't take the first one, which is if you'd like to go home, I can call you when the surgery's over and let you know how he did."

"Even if she wanted that to be an option, which I know she doesn't, neither of us has a car here," Aretha said. "Luke offered earlier to pick us up, but he won't be able to get here for at least another hour. Unless you want to call Brady."

Greg saw the answer on Nina's face as soon as Aretha said Brady's name. But before Nina could even respond, Aretha said, "You know, maybe you should call him. After all, he went with you to get Manny, and he did help you name him."

Had the two women been sitting at a dinner table, Greg thought Nina might have stretched out a leg and side-kicked her friend. This was one of those times he attempted to be invisible. The name did sound familiar to him and, if Nina knew him, most likely he worked at the magazine.

"No. He's not someone I need or want to call. I'm fine waiting for Luke." She turned to Greg. "What are the other options?"

"Well, the second one is like the first, except that instead of going home, you could go grab a coffee or something to eat, and we could call you when the surgery's over. But, since there's a car issue, looks like the third one is it. You can just hang out here."

"Then we'll take door number three. In the meantime, I'll call Luke and find out for sure when he can get here. Maybe he can bring us something to eat," Aretha said. "I'll go call him now." She bent down and whispered something to Manny, then kissed him on top of his head.

Nina stroked Manny behind his ears. "Elise told me this was your day off. I'm sure you weren't expecting a call from me . . ."

Greg checked the IV drip in Manny's paw and glanced at Nina out of the corner of his eye. *No, not expecting. But if we hadn't had a rough second start, I wouldn't have minded if you did.* "That would have been a surprise."

"I appreciate your taking time away from your family . . ." she said, adjusting the warming blanket around Manny. "I've never bothered to ask you if you have a family, beyond Elise, I mean. The last time we saw each other, I said some awful things to you."

He nodded. That was a truth they both knew couldn't be diminished.

"I shouldn't have been so mean, and I'm sorry for that. That you're here helping Manny, after the way I've treated you, is humbling. I owe you. I really do."

"Well, you can pay me back by taking me out to dinner one night. Just as a way of clearing things up between us, that's all. And beyond that, you'll just owe the emergency hospital," he said.

Tessa opened the door. "Dr. Cadoree is here."

"Great. That's the orthopedic doctor I called, so we're ready to start."

He saw that cloak of fear and love wrap itself around her when it was her turn to whisper in Manny's ear and kiss the top of his head.

Greg prayed, as she walked out, that he would not disappoint her again.

24

Luke arrived with food from Le Madeleine and the information on the person who hit Manny.

"Driver was a seventeen-year-old who was supposed to be in school, but he decided not going would be much more fun." Luke explained as they sat in the employee break room while he handed out the containers of spinach salads and croissants stuffed with chicken salad. "He was on his way to his girlfriend's house. He thought he might have missed the dog, but when he heard Aretha scream, he knew he didn't. In typical kid fashion, he got scared and left. And go figure. He went to school and checked in late."

"How could he think he missed Manny? He didn't feel the tire hit something?" Nina pushed every word out with commando force.

Luke shook his head. "I don't know. He

probably doesn't want to think about it, especially now that we found him. So, now he's dealing with an Animal Cruelty Law and his parents."

"Nina and I want him to crawl on his hands and knees over small rocks for at least five miles, but I don't think Texas has that law. What happens to him?" Aretha stabbed the strawberries in her salad and transferred them to Luke's.

"Could get up to a year in jail and a $4,000 fine. It's his first offense, probably probation, community service, maybe even require him to have some psychological counseling," said Luke.

Nina drummed her fingers on the table and stared into space while she thought. "Can he work in an animal shelter as community service? That's what he needs to do, and he should have to pay for Manny's surgery."

"That, I'm not sure of. Not bad ideas though." Luke answered Nina, but he watched Aretha as she picked through her spinach salad.

"Not so crazy about bacon, either," she said and continued her hunt.

"I'll remember for next time," he said.

She patted his hand and smiled. "I'd rather a next time with strawberries and bacon, than no next time without it."

When they walked back into the reception area, they were greeted by a little girl wearing a bright purple T-shirt decorated with fuchsia butterflies that tucked into a sequined layered purple tutu.

"Hi. Do you like to dance? I have music," she said, her eyes as shiny as her sequins. She pressed the button on the CD player she carried and twirled several times along the row of chairs.

"We're too old to twirl," Aretha told her. "But you're a cutie pie. Why don't you dance, and we'll sit and watch?"

She abandoned twirling in favor of moves that matched the reggae music she listened to and lip-synced the lyrics.

Nina didn't see any other adults except for Tessa who wasn't watching the performance. She leaned over to Aretha and whispered, "The kid looks perfectly content, but I don't think she drove here alone."

Aretha spoke as softly and pointed, "I think her mom's walking in now."

The young woman who opened the door exuded calmness. Nina felt it ripple through the room as soon as she entered. Dressed in knife-pleated jeans and a white peasant blouse, she still managed to appear almost regal. "I found your book," she said and handed the little girl a book with a green-bodied, red-headed caterpillar inching across the cover. But before she let it go, she asked, "Now, what do you say when someone has done something nice for you?"

"We say, tank you, and . . . you say . . ." The child hugged her book and leaned toward the woman.

"You are welcome." Nina smiled as the little girl placed the book and the CD player in the empty chair next to where Aretha sat. "I'm going to Miss Tessa."

Aretha said to the child, "You are beautiful just like your mommy."

The little girl tilted her head and looked wide-eyed at Aretha. "You know my mommy?"

"Well, I don't know her yet. But when she comes back, I can meet her."

She shook her head from side-to-side, her expression, serious. "No, you can't." She opened the book, then looked at Aretha. "She not here."

Aretha attempted a quick recovery and pointed to the young woman speaking to Tessa. "Oh. I thought she was your mommy."

Nina tapped Aretha on the shoulder and murmured, "Maybe you should just stop there. Otherwise —"

"Miss O'Malley, Dr. Hernandez is on his way out to talk to you," Tessa said.

Nina started to put on the shoes she'd kicked off when Greg walked out into the reception area.

"Daddy!" The little girl closed the cover of her book and, with her tutu bouncing, skipped across the room to Greg.

Nina almost dropped the shoe she held as she watched Greg.

"How's my princess?" He lifted her, kissed her forehead, and lowered her to the floor. "Daddy's almost finished, okay?"

Aretha looked at Nina. "Well, who knew?"

Nina would have preferred sprawling out in the back of Luke's SUV for the ride home. Instead, she sat in the second seat and tried to use the middle armrest and cup holder as a pillow. "I'm just too tall to make this happen." She groaned in defeat, closed her eyes, and settled for the headrest.

Thanks to Greg, she'd be able to sleep tonight. Manny's fractured left leg, not his pelvis, was all that required surgery. When he told them, Aretha rubbed Manny's head and said, "No problem. He uses his right hand anyway." But Greg also said there might be nerve damage to the leg, but that would have to be a wait-and-see situation.

Nina didn't want to leave until Manny opened his eyes. When he did, the thread of fear inside her unraveled and fell out of every muscle it seemed to have taken residence in. She knew she'd never see Greg the same way now that his unselfish heart and capable hands saved her pet. She didn't tell him that, of course. Besides, she realized as she relaxed against the headrest, she forgot to ask for a number where she could contact him.

"I'm very confused with this Greg and child situation. Nina, are you awake?" Aretha stretched her arm over the front seat and tapped Nina's knee.

She answered without opening her eyes. "Am now."

"If that lovely woman isn't that child's mother, then who is?"

"You were there, too. Why didn't you ask him?" Nina wished Aretha had asked because she wondered the same thing. If he was in a relationship with that woman, then Nina needed to stop feeling gooey inside when he shook her hand or accidentally brushed past her. Even in her anger the night of the benefit, she realized how incredibly handsome he looked. And his being unaware of his own good fortune in the way his features ended up so well-placed on his face made him even more attractive.

"For the same reason you didn't. How would that have gone? 'Thanks Dr. Hernandez for saving our pet's life. Now, where did this child come from and how is that beautiful woman related to her?' Why wouldn't we think that was her mother? Two white people do not have a black child. Maybe there's an anomaly somewhere, but . . ."

Luke cleared his throat. "May I interrupt? Why do the two of you care so much about Dr. Hernandez's marital status?"

Aretha and Nina exchanged glances.

"That's a good question," said Nina and leaned back against the headrest, closed her eyes, and waited for Aretha to announce they were home.

Greg called Elise and updated her on Manny's status as he, Paloma, and Jazarah were on their way to Marble Slab for ice cream. "Nina is meeting me at the hospital before she goes to the office tomorrow morning. While I'm checking her dog, at least she can spend some time with him."

"That was a nice thing you did, making yourself available."

"That's my job. Animal repair and maintenance," he said. "I'm just grateful he's going to make it because if he didn't, she'd be

222

convinced for life that I'm the enemy."

"I don't even pretend to understand why she would think that about you. But, I suppose that's part of what you're going to explain to me later, right? Now, go have ice cream and enjoy yourself."

The next morning, Greg arrived at the hospital to find both Nina and Aretha in the waiting room. Nina looked rested, the puffy-eyed redness of yesterday replaced by clear, deep brown eyes. Her face softened by layers of curls that rested just below her cheekbones. She smiled when she saw him, an unexpected reaction that warmed him like his first cup of coffee on a cold morning.

"Good to see both of you more relaxed today," he said as he shook hands with Nina and Aretha. He was as glad to see Nina as she was to see him. *Not so fast, buddy. Maybe she's just happy because she'll be able to visit her dog now that you're here.* "Manny's a popular guy this morning," Greg said as he moved his stethoscope from his lab pocket to around his neck.

"I didn't remember until we were home that I left my car at the office. Fortunately, Aretha has time to drop me off, but she has to get to class, so I won't be able to stay long," Nina explained.

"No problem. A quick visit is probably best anyway. An ER for the four-legged is just as unpredictable as one for the two-legged," said Greg. "Manny's over here," he walked behind the reception area and opened the door marked "Visitor Room."

"He looks so small in there," said Nina, her voice as soft as the blankets on which Manny had been placed.

Manny's tail thumped as soon as he heard Nina's voice. His face looked like it had just bloomed out of a clear plastic cone edged in felt.

Nina bent down to stroke his nose. "Does he really need this? It seems so uncomfortable."

"Those Elizabethan collars —"

"Wait," Aretha halted Greg's explanation with a wave of her hand. "As in Queen Elizabeth? What's she doing in a veterinary hospital?"

"And that's why we refer to them as E-Collars . . . less explaining. But, you're right. It's named after all those high-collared ruffles women wore then. But, for pets, it's not fashion. Those collars prevent them from scratching, biting, or in Manny's case, trying to get to his IV line," said Greg.

"Well, guess that's better than finding a

224

use for those corsets. Right, Manny?" said Aretha, bending down to pet him.

"Can I take a picture of him?" Nina reached in her purse and took out her cell phone.

"Let's not make this a magazine photo spread. I hate to rush you, sister, but we need to get going or else the traffic is going to strangle me," said Aretha, keys jangling in her hand.

"Pictures are fine," Greg told Nina. "And, if you want to stay a little longer, I can drop you off at the office on my way to work. There's something I need to give Elise anyway." He had no idea what that thing was, but he'd find something.

"That okay with you, Nina?" Aretha looked at her watch.

Nina looked at Greg. "It wouldn't be out of your way?"

He wasn't certain if she wanted it to be or not. "Isn't at all. Really."

Aretha stopped fidgeting with her keys. "Great, then I'm off."

A round of good-byes, and she scurried out, leaving a cavern between him and Nina. The kind of space that, with friends, would fill with conversation. Between two people who emotionally circled one another as if in a wrestling match, it echoed.

They fumbled chatting through the few photos Nina snapped with her cell phone, while Greg made notes on Manny's chart. He gave some instructions to the veterinary technician, then excused himself to return a text and a call he'd received earlier.

"By the time you finish, Manny will probably be ready for me to go anyway," she said.

He didn't recognize the telephone number that showed on his phone, but the text originated from the same place. They were both from Dr. Percy Maxwell, who owned two hospitals, one in Houston and one in Galveston. The doctor Greg worked for at the Cypress clinic referred him to Dr. Maxwell as he'd been searching for a full-time veterinarian to join his staff. While Greg appreciated the flexibility of a relief practice, it also meant working more weekends and the strong possibility of working holidays because that's when other doctors wanted vacation time. Knowing he could be at the same clinic every day, with a schedule that would be better for spending time with Jazarah, was appealing. Not being his own boss . . . that would be the challenge. But he trusted God would lead him down the path he needed to follow, and if it meant someone else walked ahead and cleared it, well, so be it.

Greg discovered both of them graduated within four years of one another from L.S.U.'s School of Veterinary Medicine, which, Dr. Maxwell, joked would make football season less contentious. They arranged to meet Sunday afternoon, so Percy would have more time to show him the clinic and answer questions without the interruptions of the staff and clients.

So, now Greg did have something to "drop off" to Elise, this new information. He smiled. One God-incident at a time was enough to take one more step forward.

25

Nina buckled her seat belt, relieved Greg drove something roomy, with open space between the front seats. Just being alone with him created enough tension that she expected static electricity to lift her hair off her head when he opened the door to his black Volvo SUV.

Nina surveyed the leather seats, the plush interior, the built-in entertainment systems in the back headrests. "Very nice for . . ." she paused for something more diplomatic to pop into her brain than, "for what it is."

He laughed as he started the engine. "It's okay. You can say it. It's nice for an SUV." He stopped before leaving the parking lot. "I can drive through Starbucks or something on the way in, if you'd like a coffee."

"Thanks, but Michelle probably has some made at the office by now, so I'll just get a cup there." Had she been talking to Aretha she would have added, "And I'm such a klutz, I'm sure I'd be wearing half my latte on my white angora sweater." She reached into her purse to turn her cell phone back on. "I appreciate the extra time with Manny. It was so strange walking into my house last night, not hearing him yelp or his nails clicking against the floor." Nina stopped. "Good grief, that sounds more melodramatic than I thought it would."

"Not at all. I understand."

When he glanced at her, Nina sensed that he truly did. "Speaking of high drama . . . I never did thank you for the quilt you sent to my office. Before all this happened with Manny, I intended to get in touch so I could reimburse you. I wanted to give it to Aretha for her birthday, so I don't think you should have to pay for my gift to her."

"You know, now that I've spent time around Aretha, I see why you thought of her when you saw it. She's quirky with attitude . . . and style." He took the exit off the freeway to Nina's office. He smiled. "But, I know a better way you can pay me back."

Nina's rapid blinking must have radiated the heat that just caused a reddish flush on his face. "Excuse me?"

"Whoa, talk about something not sounding like you thought it would. What I should have said was, instead of reimbursing me, why don't you send a check to We Care for whatever you would have bid? I'd probably have done that with the money you would have given me, anyway. This way, the benefit . . . benefits," he said and grinned.

"Okay, clever." That did make sense, especially since she considered he might not have told her what his final bid actually was. "You were right. Your idea is better. I'll mail them a check this week."

"But don't think I let you off the hook for that dinner. Just let me know when and where."

"I'm sure I owe you an entire banquet for what you're not charging me to take care of Manny. I don't expect you to lose money taking care of him."

He eased into a parking spot in the garage and looked at Nina. "I'm not, but I appreciate your saying that. For me, it's a chance to pay it forward. There have been times where people have reached out to help me, and those unexpected blessings made a huge difference in my life. God's making it possible right now for it to be my turn."

Nina's conscience squirmed at the mention of blessings and God. As yet, no one convinced her that a few lucky breaks meant God orchestrated them. Her brother dying, her bizarre relationship with her parents . . . were God's arms long enough to reach out to help with those? And, if they were, why hadn't He? *A conversation for another day or month or year, Nina* "Then, I suppose I can start my own paying forward with dinner. I'll check my calendar, send you a few dates that work, and you can pick the day and the place."

"I should leave the place up to you. I don't do dinner out much, so I'm not all that familiar with where to go." Greg checked the time on his cell phone. "Guess it's time for you to start reporting. I'm glad this worked out . . . being able to talk."

Nina opened the door, but Greg still hadn't turned off the engine. "Aren't you going up, too? To see Elise?"

"Oh, I, you know, this is probably a busy time for her, and I didn't warn her I was coming. I'll call her. Not like I can't find her outside of her office."

He looked like a man who'd just been caught by his office mates doodling a woman's name in his planner. She decided to leave him with his dignity. "Of course. When I see her, I'll tell her you didn't want to disturb her." Nina eased out of the leather seat. "Thanks so much for the ride. Talk to you soon."

"No problem. Glad to help. And, um," he shifted to reverse, "you have a good day."

As he drove off, Nina was proud of herself for not asking him if he'd really needed to see his sister. She was pretty sure she knew the answer to that question. And it made her smile.

Checking her text messages as she exited the elevator, Nina might have worn Brady's coffee had he not called her name in time to avoid the collision.

"Nina, where have you been?" He sounded like a teacher who'd just nabbed kids lurking in the hall during class. Carrying what was atypical for Brady, a leather briefcase, he rather looked like he was on his way to school, too.

"I'm sorry. I didn't know it was your turn to watch me." She slipped her phone back into her purse and checked the front of her sweater to be sure she escaped splatters. "Why does almost every encounter between us have to involve coffee or cameras? Anyway, you're the one who fell off the planet since I last saw you headed to the HR office."

"About that . . . well, first, what's this Elise tells me about Manny? Why didn't you call me?"

Nina moved to the side, away from the elevator traffic. "Do we have to stand here? I'm hoping Michelle made coffee, I need to check in with Shannon . . ."

"I have some time, and I needed to talk to you anyway. But let's sit in the conference room where we'll have some privacy."

She didn't expect, when they finally sat at the boat-shaped table, the mahogany gleaming with polish, that it might be the last time she'd see Brady sitting there.

"Did you just tell me you're quitting, as in no longer working here?" Nina wiggled her high-back chair closer to the table. "You're leaving *Trends*?" She turned her coffee mug in her hands, and looked at Brady. "I'm confused."

"I know. For a while, I was too. The past few weeks, I learned an important lesson. Be careful what you ask for, because you might get it." One side of his mouth went up, like he just got his own joke. "I thought I wanted New York —"

"Wait," Nina said. "*You* wanted New York? I thought you wanted Janie, and *she* wanted New York for you." She leaned back, sipped her coffee, and waited.

He moved a hand across the grain in the table. "That's harsh," he said, but his tone wasn't accusing. "But you're right. And that's why I came back. It's hard to live someone else's dream. I thought once I was in Manhattan, I'd get caught up in it. But the tornado skipped right over me."

"So, what was your fascination with me when you returned?"

Brady cast his eyes down and when he looked up, he reminded her of a child on the verge of confession. "I owe you an apology for that. Not that I meant to use you. I thought, maybe, after I figured out what I didn't want, I needed to revisit my other decisions."

Nina swiveled in the chair. "Hmm . . . then you're telling me you wanted to make sure leaving me wasn't a mistake, too?" She eyed him over the rim of the cup as she finished her coffee. "I'm flattered," she said in a way that indicated she wasn't at all.

His mouth opened, but his thoughts never made their way out because he pressed his lips together. His cell phone scuttled across the table, the vibration sounding like humming metal. He checked the number. "That one can go to voicemail." He turned to Nina. "If you're really honest with yourself, you know the mistake would have been to stay together. Assuming that would have been possible at all." He grinned. "Though I know I'm so handsome, Brad Pitt won't be seen in my presence for fear of being overshadowed."

She knew he was right. She liked the idea of a relationship with Brady more than a relationship with Brady himself, and she didn't like feeling that she lost to Janie. *And since when did competition and a trophy enter into loving someone?* "You're right. About all of it. But, honestly, it's taken your not being around for me to arrive at that conclusion. Except for the Brad Pitt thing. I would have said Channing Tatum."

Brady looked relieved. "I didn't want to leave unless we'd straightened this out between us."

"Done. Now what?"

"I've always wanted to freelance, but I liked the security of being here. If New York did anything positive, it showed me it was time for me to go after my own dream. That's what I've been talking about to Elise and HR. I'm not leaving Houston. I'm going out on my own."

"Good for you. You're a talented photographer, and I'm proud of you for going after this. I hope Elise can throw some work your way . . . speaking of which, I was counting on you for my feature," Nina said. "Has Elise said anything to you about that? I'd hate to have to break in somebody new, especially since I've already been branded with your camera lens on my forehead."

"Funny. She did, and that's the other thing I needed to mention. Since I was still on the payroll when she approved the series, she's given me the go ahead to finish it out with you. You'll need to let me know your schedule and how this is going to roll out."

Nina checked her calendar. "There's a meeting this Sunday afternoon. I'll email you the information. Can you make it?"

Brady scrolled through his phone. "Booked it. Oh, and speaking of emails . . . you'll be getting one from Janie soon. Seems like there aren't e-UNinvites. Party cancelled this weekend. You're free Saturday night."

Nina opened her calendar. *I'm free every Saturday night.*

26

Nina meant to call her mother about Manny's accident, but dread and busyness kept her from it. Not that her mother would be all that interested in his misfortune, but Nina wasn't going to leave him to go to her parents' house for lunch on Sunday. Especially if it meant going somewhere she didn't want to go. Every dinner there was like going for an annual checkup. You knew it was going to be miserable, but you had to go through it to get past it. But this time, her mother would be caught off-guard by Nina's pre-emptive strike call, so she wouldn't have as many prepared sighs and guilt trip vouchers as usual.

"Nina, something must be wrong or else you wouldn't be calling me. Right?"

"Hello, mother. How are you?"

"Are you really calling to find out how I am . . . because you usually don't bother."

I don't bother because of this exact conver-

sation. "I won't be there for dinner this Sunday. Manny, my dog, was hit by a car, and his leg's fractured. It's hard for him to get around, so he needs someone with him."

A long sigh. "So, you're choosing a dog over your parents?"

"No, mother. I'm choosing to stay home because Manny needs help right now. You and dad are welcome to come eat over here." Nina cringed hearing the words that escaped from her mouth. *What did I just say? Please don't agree. Please don't agree.*

Silence.

"Mother? Did you hear me?"

"Yes, but I am surprised that you invited us. You know your father is more comfortable watching his own television."

So, a father can choose a television over his daughter?

"Well, unless he can bring the television here, I guess we won't be seeing one another."

"You know, your brother's birthday is next month. He would have been thirty-two. Your father would want you here, you know."

"Of course he would." *But not you?* "It shouldn't be a problem. By then, Manny should be back on his own four feet." She felt her mother's eye-roll through the phone.

"We'll be expecting you then."

238

Most times after a conversation with her mother, Nina had enough pent-up frustration to heave places against the wall like Frisbees. Today she could have gone through a place setting for twelve.

"You're kidding? You rode in the car with that man, and you didn't ask him about his daughter or that woman with her?" Aretha carried a bowl of still steaming popcorn to Luke on the sofa. She handed him the bowl and plopped next to him. "Baby, that's job security right there. You won't ever have to worry about Nina out-detective-ing you."

" 'Detective-ing'? Did you just invent that word?" Luke laughed and grabbed a handful of popcorn.

"Between you looking at Aretha like she just invented a new language and the smell of that butter wafting from the kitchen, I might need Pepto-Bismol," said Nina. "And, as for my sloppy detective work, I'll have you know that there was no wedding ring on his left hand. There wasn't even a tan mark where one would have been. But, nothing we discussed transitioned into asking about his daughter."

"I know this much. If he was attached to that woman with his daughter, I doubt if he would have agreed to the two of you having dinner. He doesn't seem like the kind of man who would be unfaithful," Luke shared between bites.

"You're the hotshot detective. Why don't you and Nancy Drew come along?" Nina slipped her iPad into her portfolio, then reached in the refrigerator for a bottle of water.

"If we go with you, how will we ever be alone?" Aretha elbowed Luke who rewarded her with a kiss on her forehead.

"Exactly," said Nina. "Which is why, while I go meet the quilt people, you two are going to the clinic for visiting time with Manny. Greg said he'll release him Monday."

"We should get him a homecoming happy. A new squeaky rubber ball. He loves the ones that look like basketballs," Aretha said as she carried the empty popcorn bowl back into the kitchen.

"Let's leave now, so we'll have time to swing by a pet store after we visit. I have to get back for late shift. And if I don't wash my hands first, they'll be sliding all over the steering wheel from all that butter," said Luke.

"Isn't he adorable?" Aretha said as she watched him amble into the kitchen.

Nina smiled. "If I have to say so myself."

■ ■ ■ ■

Probably because of her smarty-pants attitude about her GPS when she spoke to one of the quilters a few days ago, Nina drove right past her destination. Faith Church and the Fellowship Hall perched on a corner at the edge of a hodge-podge residential neighborhood. A stand of pine trees obscured the front of the white-bricked Fellowship Hall, so when she turned around, she had to trust that the GPS voice telling her she'd arrived at her destination was directionally smarter. It was. Nina didn't see Brady's car. She hoped he remembered.

At the door, she didn't know whether she should knock or just walk in, so she did a combination of the two. "Is this the Threads of Hope group?" she asked once inside. Had she surveyed the room for thirty seconds, the question would have been unnecessary.

Bolts of fabric draped several of the long tables on one side of the room. On the other side, four tables surrounded by chairs had been pushed together and held pieces of fabric, scissors, and rulers of all shapes and sizes.

A young woman with a shoulder-length

waterfall of sand-shaded ringlets walked out of one of the side rooms. She set the bundle of clothes she carried on a chair. "You must be Nina. I talked to you on the phone," the young woman shook Nina's hand.

"Crystal. Yes, I remember. Nice to meet you." After their first conversation, Nina expected to meet someone barely out of her teens, but Crystal looked not much younger than she was.

"Come on in, I'll show you around and introduce you to everyone. They should all be here soon."

By the time Brady arrived, Nina had met Crystal's mother Kelley, the hospice nurse Becca, Pam, Lacey, and Jenny. "There are more people here sometimes, but since we just finished the quilts for the We Care benefit, we're just working on designs right now," Kelley explained.

Nina introduced Brady and, while he snapped pictures, she explained the feature series, her idea to spotlight the different people involved and bring attention to The AIDS Memorial Quilt and their group's contributions. "Of course, I'll need your permission, and I understand you might need to think about it first, so you don't need to give me a decision today."

"Actually, Crystal had told us about the

feature part. We talked about it already, and we all want to help. If our stories can make a difference, we want to tell them," said Pam, who joined Becca as she cut squares from the stack of clothes Crystal plopped on the table. "There're two more people who usually come, but they're both going to be late. We hadn't talked to them yet, so if you'll still be here, you can ask them, too."

"Great," said Nina, adding more notes. "What are their names?"

"Martha is one. She's just running late today. The other one had an appointment, so we're not sure when he'll make it. His name is Dr. Hernandez, but we just call him Greg."

27

Greg left his meeting with Dr. Maxwell and called Elise. He wanted to tell her about the interview before he arrived at the quilting group. "I'm going back on one of the clinic days, and that will tell me a lot about the practice as well. But, I'm thinking this could be a blessing. It's close to the house, and the owner is someone I really think I can work with."

"I'll add it to the prayer list," she said. "Do you realize the older we get, the longer the list is?"

"And with that, I'm calling Paloma," he said. She and Jazarah were making cookies. He pictured the kitchen decorated with chips and icing and his daughter probably finger-painting with cookie dough. That was a mess he didn't mind missing right now.

It was later than usual when Greg arrived at the fellowship hall, so he was surprised to see so many cars still in the parking lot. He opened the door and saw a man taking pictures. And Nina. *Nina?*

She smiled when she saw him. "Don't worry, I looked like you do now when they told me you were actually a part of this group," she said. "I didn't know, of course, that night at the benefit that you actually designed the quilt I liked. You're a man of many talents, Dr. Hernandez."

And you're a woman who continues to surprise me. Which he might have actually said had he not been distracted by the scent of gardenias that lingered after she'd reached out and patted his shoulder. "See, I'm not just another pretty face, am I?" he said, but Nina didn't participate in his smiling. Greg saw the way her eyes searched his face, and he realized it wasn't a joke to her. It was exactly what she thought of him. Ever since high school.

She looked at him and, like someone who'd just decided to participate in the auction bidding, nodded. "My eyesight must have improved over the years. I see exactly what you mean," she said and mirrored his grin with her own. "Okay, time to exude your boyish charm for the camera. I want you to meet Bracy."

Greg recognized him as soon as he introduced himself. The man driving the white convertible the night of the benefit. The convertible with Nina in the passenger seat.

"I photographed quilts the night of the benefit. Your group's quite talented," said Brady.

"Thanks," Greg replied, "I'm blessed to be surrounded by creative people. Who make cookies and keep me coming back."

The women at the table laughed. Brady walked over to Nina who was examining some quilts in progress. Greg watched Brady and Nina. Actually, he watched Brady watch Nina as she pointed to places around the room. Could he have missed some connection between the two? A connection more than a reporter and photographer? He waited as they spoke and looked for those suggestions of intimacy between a couple. Hands, eyes, laughter that lingered, or the space between them narrowing as if drawn together by their sheer magnetism. Greg witnessed none of those between the two, and the relief he experienced was its own signal.

Greg joined Brady and Nina. He reminded himself to focus on the conversation and not the tilt of her head when she asked a question or the curve of her waist as she held a square up to examine or how she used her thumb to twirl the pearl ring on her ring finger as she spoke.

The three of them walked around the room. Greg showed them patterns, sample squares, bolts of fabric, and pictures that had been taken of other quilts they'd sewn. "One of the goals we're working on is to make a panel for everyone in the group who's lost someone to AIDS. It's taking a while longer than we expected because we work on those when we can. But it gives the group time to save money for another goal. We hope to be able to personally deliver those squares to D.C."

"Impressive," said Brady. "You know, a friend of mine, someone I grew up with, died of AIDS five years ago. I don't know if they've ever thought of creating a panel for him."

Crystal's mother, Kelley, sitting nearby, turned to Brady. "Didn't mean to be eavesdropping, but there is a way for you to find if there's already a panel for your friend."

"Thanks, but if you mean going to a display, I don't have time —"

"No. No. You don't have to travel at all. Watch," Kelley said and asked Nina if she could use her iPad. "Even the Quilt is joining the 21st century. Look." She showed them the web app that people can use to browse the entire collection of panels and even read personal stories.

"What a great sidebar this will be for the first profile," Nina said.

"Guess I need a tech training session. I didn't realize you were so app-aware, Kelley," Greg said as he bookmarked the site on his cell phone.

"I'm not," Kelley said as she pointed to her daughter. "Crystal's the one who's always searching and researching." She tucked the ringlets that curtained her daughter's face behind as ears as Crystal steered her scissors around yellow and orange flowers on what was once a skirt.

"Because if I didn't," Crystal said as she moved the skirt into a basket of other shorn clothes, "you would still be using a cell phone the size of a shoe box."

"True," Kelley said and helped her daughter spread out a large chintz curtain.

Brady took a few more shots, then left after he and Nina scheduled a series of interview times. Greg scanned the list she showed him. "You didn't ask me," he said.

"You're right. Interviewing the person who helps design all these quilts would be another angle." Nina opened her calendar.

"Is that what I am? An angle?" Greg shook his head as if dismayed by the revelation.

"Sorry, Miss O'Malley, but you have it all wrong."

Nina's eyes drilled into him. "I what?"

"I'm not your angle," he said. Greg knew he was about to learn more about Nina O'Malley than she would learn about him. "Jazarah, my daughter, is the angle. She's HIV-positive."

Sitting in Carraba's, the one restaurant that Nina could think of in a stunned state, she looked across the table at Greg as he listened to a voicemail about one of his patients. She wanted to tell him that she didn't mind at all that he had a pretty face. In fact, she wondered why this man, who walked into a room and women knew he was there, might be interested in her. *Or, Nina, maybe he's not. Being nice to someone doesn't equal a relationship.*

When Nina heard his daughter's name, she felt like that spinning beach ball that appeared when a program on her laptop wasn't processing information. Greg not only had a daughter, she was Ethiopian and HIV-positive. Nina realized that everything she thought she knew about Greg was about to be redefined.

When her belated response to him was, "I'm confused," he told her he understood.

And that's when he suggested dinner, so he could, as he said, "unconfuse" her.

The waitress, whose name badge read "Roxie," brought their meals, grilled salmon with tomato basil vinaigrette for him and tilapia with garlic for Nina. When Greg thanked her, she flashed him a lipsticked smile that could have melted pats of butter. "Need anything else?" She didn't even pretend to look at Nina.

"I'd appreciate a refill," said Nina and held up her iced tea glass.

Roxie barely turned in her direction. "Sure, I'll be right back." She picked up the glass like she was taking it in the kitchen to dust for fingerprints and strolled off.

Nina laughed when she walked away. "I think Roxie would like for you to be quite needy."

"Really? Why?" He handed Nina the bread basket.

"You're oblivious. It's endearing," said Nina. "So, tell me about your daughter. Who, by the way, oozes personality." A quality that definitely could have connected her genetically to Greg.

"She does, doesn't she? Makes me think that in ten or so years, I'm going to have to be quite a vigilant father." He smiled and, though he looked at Nina, it was as if a picture of his daughter was behind her. "We brought her home, underweight and under-developed, and depended on prayer and love. And, so far, it's working."

Nina ate a few bites of her tilapia contemplating how to send the train of their conversation down a different track so she could ask about his wife. Maybe the divorce was messy, maybe she cheated on him, or maybe she was home scraping his uneaten dinner down the waste disposal. The suggestion of that discombobulated her and sent her fork to her plate in a noisy landing.

Of course, Roxie appeared with her fresh glass of iced tea at that moment, and Nina could almost hear Roxie's brain telegraphing Greg, "Oh, you're such a kind man to participate in Take a Klutz to Dinner night." Roxie set Nina's glass on the table, then let her eyes linger on Greg for a while and announced she'd return later with a dessert menu. *Hoping I'll order something so calorie-evil, I'll need a different size dress to leave the restaurant.*

Nina, you're a journalist. If you can't ask the hard questions, Elise will assign you to Cub Scout banquets. First, she put her fork down, then she spotted Roxie serving a table of eight, she knew she couldn't wait or else she'd be detailing the ingredients of

251

every dessert on the menu to Greg. She plunged in. "Did things not work out between you and your wife?"

Greg's reaction came in waves, starting with surprise, then confusion, then he sat back in his chair as if pushed there by the force of her question. He looked down at the table, but when his eyes met Nina's, she heard the sad understanding of his response, "When you live with something for a long time, you start to assume everyone knows." Greg placed his napkin on his now bare plate. "Lily died in an automobile accident right before Jazarah's second birthday."

She was about to say she was sorry when a memory rushed forward, pulled by the weight of his words. The night of the benefit, her angry retort, "I prayed pain would bury itself in you," and his reply that she no longer needed to utter that prayer. If shame had its own taste, it coated her mouth like mucous. The horror of her arrogance spilled out of her eyes and trembled in her hands. Her heart's voice couldn't be heard above the deafening roar of regret.

Before she could speak, Greg silenced everything in her that screamed at her own meanness. He reached across the table, his hand quieting hers. "Nina, you didn't know. You didn't know."

With her other hand she blotted her face with her napkin "That's not an excuse for . . ."

"You're right, it's not. But I forgive you, I really do."

"Forgive me? How can you? I don't deserve forgiveness —"

"If we deserved it, it wouldn't be forgiveness. And I can do this because God does it for me. Sometimes on a daily basis."

28

Nina left the table to rid herself of "the black streams of tears" flowing down her face. Greg called Paloma and asked if it would be a problem if he was home later than he anticipated.

His nanny laughed. "Dr. Hernandez, you do not have a curfew, but I am glad you called. Jazarah saved you cookies, and she put them on the fireplace. 'Like Santa,' she said. So you must eat them . . . or something . . . so they will be gone when she awakes."

He promised he would and told her he'd be home within the next two hours.

"Are you still at the quilting meeting?" She sounded concerned that he might be.

"No, I'm having dinner with a friend, Nina O'Malley. Her dog, Manny, is the one I got the ER call about when we were on our way to lunch. If fact, she was in the waiting room the same time you and the little princess were. Tallish, short dark hair." He looked up to see Nina ease into her chair, then tuck her bangs behind her ear, only to have them slide back down. A familiar gesture, one he used to see in Lily whenever she felt self-conscious. Greg smiled at her, then realized he had no idea what Paloma had said. "I'm sorry, could you repeat that."

"Have a good time, Dr. Hernandez."

"I already am. Thanks." He ended the call, and Roxie appeared at his elbow asking about coffee and a dessert menu. They both ordered coffee and, to their waitress's disappointment, passed on dessert.

Roxie delivered the two coffees, telling Greg she'd "be delighted, for sure" to provide him refills, and swayed away.

"Is it painful? To talk about her, I mean. Lily must have been a remarkable woman to open her heart to adopt an HIV-positive child."

Greg leaned forward, hands clasped on the table, and smiled. "No, not now. After she died, people sometimes apologized if her name came up in conversation or, worse, didn't talk about her at all. As if she never existed."

His neighbors Dale and Amelia, whose son died of cancer at the age of twenty-eight, understood the importance of not smothering the memories of loved ones under blankets of silence. Greg knew it was that empathy that drew him to involvement in the We Care benefit and supporting The AIDS Memorial Quilt.

Every panel represented a family sharing and celebrating the life of someone they loved. Greg told Nina about Lily's passion for life, how when she loved, she gave it all away. Her drive to bring Jazarah home sometimes drove a wedge between them because when she decided to go after something, she was not going to be denied. Greg would argue, when the paperwork and the politics overwhelmed the process, that maybe they should wait or try to adopt in the states.

One night, she must have printed copies of the picture she'd taken in New York of the quilt panel of the five-month-old little girl who died of AIDS. When he woke up the next morning, they were taped all over the house. On his bathroom mirror, the refrigerator, doors, cabinets. Even the rearview mirror of his car. He'd walked back inside that day, wrapped his arms around her waist, and whispered, "You win. There's a baby waiting for us to pray her home."

They prepared themselves for having an

HIV-positive child by talking to other families and reading whatever they could find that would help. They knew the virus could impair her immune system's ability to control viral infections, bacterial lung and ear infections. But they also knew she would have a normal life expectancy because modern drug therapies made the virus almost undetectable. A week after starting her antiretroviral therapy, her virological suppression was at 90 percent. Within a month, it was 99 percent.

"Ironic. Lily spent so much time and energy doing all she could to make sure Jazarah would live, and she was the one who died."

On her way to the office on Monday, Nina received two texts from Greg. One asked her to call him to discuss Manny going home. The other, saying how much he enjoyed their time together, asked if she had plans for Saturday She smiled, remembering him walking her to her car after dinner. How no matter how old you are, there's that geeky awkwardness of saying good night to someone you're attracted to, which resulted in a clumsy kiss somewhere between her lips and her ear. For Nina, it was enough to let her know, she'd try again.

Dinner with Greg had trumped the anxiety of Daisy returning, so that walking to her desk, Nina was surprised by the familiar scent of rain, which meant she was back. Her earth-friendly accessories surrounding her as before, Daisy settled in as if she'd never left.

"Nina, I'm so excited to see you," said Daisy, springing from her chair, her shock of sprouting hair now gathered into a neat bun at the nape of her neck.

Setting her briefcase on the floor, Nina hugged Daisy, who seemed smaller and frailer than she remembered. "I'm glad you're here, but I don't know why you left in the first place," Nina said. "Now, let me look at you. Did you even eat while you were in New York?"

"I so owe you an apology. Maybe several. You deserve an explanation. Do you have time to talk now?"

"Let me find Shannon. She's been helping me, and doing a bang-up job at it, too. I'll be back."

After getting notes from her intern, who proved her savvy by delegating some of the work to another intern, Nina returned to her desk. "Did you want to talk here?"

"Here is fine." Daisy scooted her chair around the partition. "I'm going for the condensed version because, well, I'm exhausted. My flight was late yesterday, and I didn't get to bed until after midnight, so I might not be too coherent."

"We don't have to do this now —"

"No, I want to. I've wanted to since I left." She kicked off her sandals and sat, cross-legged on the chair, her cotton skirt pulled over her knees. "Here's what happened . . ."

Daisy's mother had moved to New York months before with a man who promised he'd marry her as soon as he started his job there. The job started, but the marriage didn't. "My mother called, hysterical, that she wants to move out, but she doesn't want to be homeless again. And then she pummels me with guilt about her being all alone, no one to help her . . . I talked to Elise because I thought there might be a way for me to get on staff in New York. I could get my mother situated, stay for a while, come back here . . . I told her I didn't want to step on your toes because I knew how much you wanted to be there."

Elise had called Daisy the day after Janie made her grand announcement to tell her there was a possible opening. But it was Elise's suggestion that Daisy not make a permanent decision until she arrived there, checked on her mother's situation, and spent time in the New York office.

"She told me she'd keep my job open here, so I didn't want to create high drama. Janie already had her production going on, but there just wasn't enough time for me to explain it all. And, if I ended up back here anyway — ta da! — then I would have put us both through that for no reason."

Daisy said that her mother lived in an apartment almost worse than the car they lived in for weeks. Janie offered to let them stay with her. "And that was the beginning of the end. My mother was making me crazy. Janie kept pressuring me to stay, mostly because I think she saw Brady slipping away. And, Nina, the New York office, is this place," she moved one out-stretched arm in a circle, "on steroids."

Nina sat straighter in her chair like someone about to be rewarded. She'd thrive in that energy.

But it debilitated Daisy. "I told my mother that if she wanted to live with family, then she needed a Houston zip code. She balked at first. I'm not even sure why, because she wasn't all that devastated leaving," she gazed at the ceiling, "I think his name was Eric. Finally, I convinced her to come back with me. She's been here less than twenty-four hours, and she's already complaining.

She's been homeless so much throughout her life that I think having what could be a real home feels strange to her."

After she and Daisy finished talking, Nina called Greg to make arrangements for picking up Manny. As she waited for him to answer, she surveyed the office. Nests of submarine gray partition walls separated the staff writers from the ad writers from the classifieds. Days closer to deadline, the nest swarmed with the energy of people moving from hive to hive, the impatient rings of telephones, the electrical current of voices that punctuated the stillness between.

Would she exchange this for the frenetic pace of the New York office? Without a doubt.

"This is Dr. Hernandez."

When he knew that she was on the other end of the line, his professional tone gave way to the one with which she had become familiar.

"Hey, Nina. How's your day going?"

"So far, so good," she answered. "Thanks for your text. I had fun, too. I'd love to get together Saturday."

"Great. We'll talk soon about that. In the meantime, can you meet me at the ER clinic around four this afternoon? We can release

Manny then, and I can go over what he'll need. He's making great progress, and I'm sure he's ready to be home."

"Aretha and I have missed the little yapper. Tell him we'll see him in a few hours."

Nina then contacted Kelley and her daughter Crystal, and they arranged to meet the next morning over breakfast.

Daisy and Nina had lunch with Elise in her office to work out story assignments. Nina arrived before Daisy and was relieved Elise made no mention of her having been with her brother. While policies existed for office romances, she had no idea how to handle a relationship with a boss's sibling. *Getting ahead of yourself, Nina. One dinner isn't a relationship, but I wouldn't mind if more did make it so.*

Elise had arranged for a local deli to provide salads and a tray of fruit, with a side of chocolate gelato. "Figured we'd be tossing ideas around, might as well toss salads, right?" She looked at Daisy and Nina. "Guess that wasn't as funny as I'd hoped."

Nina expected to play polite tug-of-war over some of the assignments. But Daisy offered to take over the political corruption story without any protest, so Nina could focus on the feature.

"But I thought you didn't like writing those stories," Nina said.

"I'm learning to stretch. Besides, you might want to get back to politics after you dabble in the wild side of feature writing," Daisy said and handed Nina her salad bowl for a refill.

Elise closed her laptop. "Sometimes life works out so much better than we anticipated," she said and smiled in Nina's direction.

29

Kelley and Crystal waved Nina to their table where they already had coffee waiting.

"After all those years of using, Carlys surprised us by not dying of a drug overdose. Never would have thought it though. That girl checked in and out of rehab hospitals like they were resort hotels."

Crystal, her twin, handed her mother a biscuit. "Except that the resorts might have cost less."

Kelley squeezed her daughter's hand. "Might be right on that one. Anyway," she breathed in as if Nina had pressed a stethoscope to her chest, "last time out, she stayed clean for months. Then, we started to notice she was sleeping longer. 'Course we were suspicious, how could we not be? But when Crystal told us about her night sweats and her complaints of fever, we figured one monster of a cold was headed her way."

The monster wreaking havoc upon Carlys

wasn't a cold. It was AIDS.

"The doctor told us she probably shared a dirty needle with someone who was infected. Of course, Carlys had no idea who that someone might be." Crystal rubbed her arms like the temperature dropped. "It's so weird to think a stranger killed my sister, and doesn't even know."

"Almost a year later, Carlys died. And she stayed clean. She was proud of herself for that. But . . ." Against a backdrop of dishes clattering, the thick smell of bacon, and the wait staff carrying trays like large brown halos, Kelley shared the pain that ripped through her every night. The wound that would never heal.

". . . people who knew Carlys, just figured it was drugs that killed her. I never told them otherwise. Couldn't make myself say my daughter died from AIDS." She looked at Nina. "What kind of mother lies about why her child died?"

When Nina returned to her office, she didn't remember eating breakfast at all.

"Do you realize that Kelley's daughter might have been saved by something that costs less than a dollar?" Nina handed Aretha the article she'd been reading on syringe exchange and needle share programs

265

and their importance in reducing and preventing HIV. "These programs provided a way for drug users to be given free sterile syringes. That one difference could have saved her from being infected."

Aretha leaned against the pine tree and propped the tablet against her knees. "I'd like to read this. Make sure Mr. Manny doesn't try to escape."

"As if," said Nina. "He's basking in the outdoors, content to be home." She carried him outside, as per Greg's instructions, for what Aretha referred to as his daily "constitutional." After their first adventure into the front yard yesterday, Aretha told Manny he needed a few less amendments to his constitution.

The sun hadn't yet disappeared into a pocket of clouds when the three of them settled on a patch a grass, the two women sitting cross-legged in front of the dog, blocking the street. Even if he had a yearning to dash in that direction, there was no way he'd outrun them. So, Manny alternately lifted his head to catch a breeze, then rested it on top of his bandaged leg.

Nina scratched behind his ears, remembering Greg's litany of instructions when they checked Manny out of the clinic. He helped Aretha settle the dog in the car while

Nina wrote a check for his treatment. Once outside, she'd thanked him for his help with Manny and with the charges. "I appreciate all you did for Manny, and I meant it when I said I didn't want this costing you more than it cost me," she told him

"Not at all. And even if it did, you . . . I mean Manny, was worth it."

Aretha was packing a dinner to take to Luke who worked late shift, and Nina had started writing her feature about Carlys when Greg called about dinner and a movie Saturday night. "Or it could be a movie and dinner, either way."

They were still talking when Aretha came back almost an hour later.

"Did you read it? What did you think?"

Elise and Peyton had stopped by Saturday on their way home from lunch to spend time with their niece, but Greg knew his sister. She didn't want to just hear his reaction to Nina's first article, she wanted to examine every pore on his face for a reaction.

Greg relocated a collection of stuffed bears from the couch to the coffee table so his sister and brother-in-law could have a place to sit. Sheets had been loosely tented on the furniture in one-half of the family room. A play kitchen, art easel, and a stack of books took up space in the other half.

"I haven't had a chance to read it yet because I've been a tent-building, water-coloring, tea-partying daddy most of the morning," Greg said as he picked two dolls and a broken cookie off the floor. "I may need to spend time at the gym to build stamina just to play with my daughter."

Peyton looked around the room. "Ever thought of putting up a train or a race track? Get one of those, and I'll join the play group."

While Peyton talked, Jazarah's little round singing could be heard coming from one of the flowered tents. "I hiding. I hiding. I hiding."

"I'll write them both on your Christmas list, Peyton," said Elise. "We'll entertain the princess. You go read that piece that Nina worked on for the past three weeks." Elise slipped out of her heels, and in a too-loud voice said, "Uncle Peyton, we have to find our little lost niece. Where could she be?"

A soft giggle floated into the room. Greg watched as his sophisticated sister and her husband crawled the short space to where Jazarah hid under a sheet draped over a chair. As Greg left the room, he heard Peyton exclaim, "There you are!" followed by the delighted squeals of his daughter.

In that moment, Greg realized God's reunion with Lily must have sounded much the same. And if what Greg experienced with his daughter was a mere shadow of what God experienced with His daughter, he knew Lily's joy was more spectacular than he could imagine.

Have fun, my sweet Lily. Fill the heavens with your laughter.

The features had started weeks ago when Nina opened her email to read one of Elise's "see me" directives. Nina closed her laptop and waited for her insides to stop practicing aerobics. At one time, the internal gut-bouncing meant she feared the dragon-lady's fire belching. Not now. Not today. The knot was her own.

"Nina, these interviews are powerful and poignant. The feedback we're receiving is incredible. Every story resonates because this disease may be pandemic, but it's personal. And you're not only telling stories, you're weaving in facts that people might not ever know or feel comfortable asking."

Elise's office door was already open when Nina arrived. As soon as she walked in, Nina eyed a stack of magazines on her desk.

"Have a seat." Elise's voice was the excited

impatience of someone waiting for a show to start. "Water?"

When Nina turned down the offer of water, Elise picked up the magazine with her first article, the one featuring Kelley's daughter Carlys, from a stack on her desk. "The information here about federal funding of needle exchange programs, the number of infections from injection drugs, is getting people's attention."

The second interview, with Pam and Eli, already parents of three biological children, told their story of finding their adopted son Jacob begging on the streets. "If Eli had not been there with the medical team, Jacob and his sister would probably have died by now. We saved two children," Pam had said, "but since 1984, over 14 million children have been orphaned in Southern Africa because of AIDS." Elise said local organizations contacted her to thank her because they'd experienced an increased interest in volunteer teams after the article published.

Nina appreciated Elise's enthusiasm, but knew if she didn't say something soon, her courage would stomp out like an unwelcome visitor. Before Elise picked up another magazine, Nina blurted, "Elise, there's another story I want to discuss with you."

Elise's eyes switched to high beams.

"Another series?" She grabbed her note-book.

Nina's body was firmly planted in the chair across from her boss, but her mind paced up and down the office. "Well, only if a series of dates would . . ." She inched forward. "I don't know why I'm trying to be clever, here. You know Greg and I have been seeing each other, and I think you and I have handled the boundaries well."

"If you consider pretending it's not hap-pening to be handling it well then I agree with you," Elise said. "Wait, I meant that to be amusing. Peyton's always telling me I don't do amusing well. I need to listen to the man more."

Nina loosened her grip on the chair arms. "Okay, I'm glad you clarified that. I just figured there would be a time when one of us would have to bring it up. And, this is it."

Elise's expression was guarded, but Nina had prepared herself for the worst. So far, the discussion was miles ahead of what she expected. "Greg wants me to meet Jazarah this weekend, and I know this is a huge step for him. I care about him very much. The challenge is, I'd love to end the series with an interview with him. But, before I ap-proached him, I wanted to talk to you. Not just because of Greg, but because of what it would mean for you as well."

Elise tapped her pen on her planner and stared out the window as she was prone to do when she wrestled with a decision. The pen slowed to a stop, and Nina saw a softer, less intense Elise. Even her eyes, usually like two dark drill bits ready to bore into someone, appeared relaxed. "Like you, I've been wondering when we'd have to cross the line from colleagues to, well, two women who care about the same man. Once we stepped over it, we'd have to be able to move back and forth, and yet not get our roles confused." She left her desk and closed the door to her office. She pulled a chair from the corner and moved it next to Nina's before she sat. "Of course, I've known you and Greg have spent time together. When he finally shared the high school and benefit night disasters, I was surprised and impressed that you both moved past that." She looked away for a moment, and then continued. "Elise, Greg's sister, who knows that she's not seen her brother this happy in a long time, has hesitated telling you this. But, Elise, your editor, knows she must."

Nina, had she been given a minute of privacy, would have checked under her chair to see if her stomach had gone there. Elise couldn't possibly be setting her up for something negative, could she? Nina wished now she'd taken her up on that offer of water earlier.

"We're pulling Janie out of New York. It's a disaster. The job is yours, if you want it."

30

Nina experienced, for the first time, that exquisite moment of dream becoming reality, when the word surreal becomes palpable, and you recognize that if this one thing is possible, then so is the second or third or anything after. She feared she might not be able to respond to Elise for the horn-blowing celebration marching through her head. "I'm happily stunned. Happily. Stunned." This time, her grip on the armrests was to prevent her from leaping out of the chair and clapping like a cheerleader.

"Of course, your discretion and confidentiality are expected at this point. And you don't need to make a decision now or even this week." Elise looked at her watch. "My cell phone, my telephone, my email will all be assaulted in the next hour after the editor talks to Janie. It's going to take a solid two weeks for movement, and I'm certain it's going to be a struggle. But it's not one you need to involve yourself in." She grabbed two water bottles out of the small refrigerator near her desk and, this time, Nina accepted one. "I want you to give this serious thought, write down any questions or concerns you have, and we'll talk next week."

Nina streamed out a chorus of, "Great. Good. Sure. Of course," as Elise spoke. She was about to thank her, when Elise said, "Oh, one more thing. And I'm going to cross that boundary, but I feel it's necessary. If and when you discuss this with Greg or tell him your decision is your call. By the time this is all finalized, should you move ahead, it might be at least three or four weeks. Getting close to Jazarah and then leaving is going to be tough. I'm not suggesting you don't meet her. Everyone should, she's an amazing kid. But, be aware that she's one of those kids who forms attachments quickly. Breaking them is tough."

"I understand. And, Elise, thank you for this chance."

"You're welcome. Just be sure it's still what you want. I have no doubt you can make it work. But remember, geography isn't a magical cure."

Stepping out of the elevator, Elise's offer

bouncing around inside her, knowing she'd been given the choice to stay or to go, Nina's vision of the office was already one degree of separation away. But the empowerment she felt inside the *Trends* office didn't transfer so easily to her life outside of it. The closer her car brought her to home, the less detached she felt about her surroundings.

She wouldn't be relocating her life as she knew it and reconstructing it in Manhattan. Aretha, her home, her Girls' Night Out group would stay in Houston. Manny? What would she do about him, especially since she had no idea where she'd live? No backyards in a high-rise to run around in. By the time she unlocked her front door, she'd already started finding the flaws in her diamond.

When Manny didn't bark at the sound of her key in the lock, Nina dropped everything and ran to the kitchen to check his crate. Once she spotted the note taped to it, her heart made its way down, and out of her throat. Aretha said she and Luke took Manny for his follow-up visit because Greg wasn't going to be at the clinic Saturday.

About to be annoyed she missed a chance to see Greg, Nina's brain kicked into gear reminding her she was the reason Greg wasn't working Saturday. They were taking Jazarah to the Butterfly Museum. And, now, having thought about being with him this weekend, she couldn't *not* think about him. Six little mini-Snickers, a handful of jelly beans, and several spoons of Blue Bell straight from the carton later, she still couldn't stop thinking about him. When the sugar therapy failed, she changed into yoga pants that had never seen the inside of a yoga studio and a T-shirt.

She decided to start doing research for her interview with Martha. In 1983, Martha and Frank drove to Women's Hospital when their son-in-law Dan called to tell them their daughter Jill was in labor and about to deliver their first grandchild. They arrived to learn Jill hemorrhaged during delivery and required a transfusion of two pints of blood, but she was stabilized and eager for them to meet their grandson, Adam. Jill nursed Adam for six months. He grew into a chunky little crawler. By the time he was a year old, he'd already started taking stiff-legged steps from one side of the room to the other.

A few years later, Martha made one of the most difficult telephone calls of her life. She'd heard a news report that said tainted blood transfusions could cause something

called acquired immune deficiency syndrome. Jill tested positive, but Dan was
negative. Adam, because he was breast-fed,
also tested positive. Frank and Martha's
grandson died at the age of six. No tested
or approved drugs for pediatric patients
with AIDS existed at that time. By 1987,
Jill was able to start taking AZT, an antiretroviral medicine that the FDA had approved.

Nine years later, Frank and Martha buried
their daughter next to her son.

Researching the progression of AIDS for
the story, Nina made notes of the three different stages. The first two were characterized as HIV, and the third and final stage of
infection is AIDS. As she clicked from one
site to verifying information and listing
symptoms, she felt like someone playing
Jeopardy!. She had the answers, but she
couldn't figure out the question.

Nina started again, thinking perhaps she'd
just missed something along the way. When
the question finally came to her, she wished
that it hadn't because once you know
something, you can't not know it. Which is
not the same as pretending you don't know,
and it was that very difference that turned
her inside-out.

Luke, carrying Manny in his crate, and

Aretha were walking toward the front door when Nina met them. "Thanks for taking Manny. I've . . . there's something I have to do. Won't be long."

"Nina, what's wrong? Something, for sure. You won't even go through a drive-through without being dressed." She turned to Luke. "Maybe I should go with her . . ."

"No. I appreciate the thought, but no. I need to do this on my own, and I'll tell you later. Just trust me."

Nina pressed the doorbell, which wasn't a bell at all. It sounded like a cattle prod. She pressed it again. And again. And again. Her parents were probably sitting within two feet of one another, each one waiting for the other to open the door.

"Hold ya horses out there."

"Dad, it's Nina. Open the door, please."

"Why, Nina, what brought you —"

"Is mom home? I need to talk to you both." She edged past her dad into the house. "Mom. Where are you?"

Sheila walked out of the kitchen, drying her hands on a frayed dishtowel. Nina recognized concern on her face, one she found at a fire sale.

"It's not Sunday. And where would you be going dressed that way?"

"I think, mother, you might want to pay more attention to my emotional cues, not my yoga pants. Should it matter how I dress to go to my parents' house? Were you expecting company?"

Her father patted his shirt pocket to check if he had his cigarettes. He quit smoking ten years ago, but the habit stayed. Especially when he felt uncomfortable or anxious. "Honey, what's going on?"

"Let's sit at the table," said Nina. "I have something I want to show you."

They sat, neither one of them taking their eyes off of her.

"I'm going to ask you a question, and I want you to tell me the truth. The real truth. Not the truth with a spin on it. Or the one you want."

"Nina, you're being —"

"Actually, Dad, I'm being Nina. The one that's been showing up at your house on Sundays? She's the lie. It's time for all of us to stop lying to one another." The way their eyes darted back and forth between themselves and Nina, the perplexed expressions? Nina considered they may not know the truth themselves. But she was about to find out.

"What really killed Thomas?" Each word held its own weight and landed on the platform of Nina's conviction.

"I can't believe my own daughter . . ." her mother pushed her chair back from the table.

Nina would have tackled her if she tried to leave the conversation. "You're not running away from this. And you didn't answer my question."

"Honey, why should she? You already know the answer," said her father, pleading like a child.

"I know what you told me. But there's more that you're not." She opened her iPad, found her notes, and handed the tablet to her parents. "Recognize those?"

Her dad reached in his empty shirt pocket. Her mother pushed the tablet back to Nina. "Do you know how much that hurts your father and me? Why are you making us look at all this? You know Thomas got sick, pneumonia, and died."

"You're not going to let go of that are you? Guess you've said it for so long, you believe it yourself." Nina closed the iPad. "For the past two months, I've been writing a series for the twenty-fifth anniversary of The AIDS Memorial Quilt. I need to research HIV and AIDS because of the families I interviewed. And there they were. It's not a coincidence that these symptoms were Thomas's symptoms. Or that you wouldn't let me go to the hospital. Or that you buried him without waiting for his friends or even some of your own relatives. Thomas died from AIDS."

She watched her parents' faces pale and shift until they bore almost the same expression Kelley's did when she said, "What kind of mother lies about why her child died?"

"We wanted to protect you," said her father. "Things were different then. Your mother and I didn't really understand or know what AIDS was until the doctor explained it to us. Even then, we were in shock."

"What did you think you were protecting me from? For all you knew, I could have used his toothbrush or shaved my legs with one of his razors . . . How was that keeping me safe?"

"Thomas made sure that didn't happen, Nina," said her mother, the exasperation evident in her voice. "We wanted to protect you from other people who might say things to you. What do you think would have happened to you at school if people knew your brother died from AIDS? Especially all those years ago, before people with HIV lived for decades. Even today, some people think you get AIDS from hugging or swimming or sharing food. What do you think

282

people said then?"

"I don't know. But Thomas was my only sibling, and I never had a chance to tell him good-bye." Nina didn't try to stop herself from crying. "Were you ever going to tell me?"

Her parents looked at each other. Her father clasped his hands on the table "I don't think so. We didn't want it to change the way you saw your brother."

"Why because of the AIDS or that he was gay or both?"

Nina's father leaned back in his chair and stared at his daughter. For the first time in years, Nina witnessed the man inside the shell he'd become. 'If you don't believe us, I guess I would understand. But your brother wasn't gay. His first year in college, his friends made fun of him because he was a virgin. They all went out drinking one night, and the next morning he wasn't alone in his room. She called him three months later to tell him she'd tested positive for AIDS.

"Guess you can understand how easy it is to make assumptions about people with HIV and AIDS. Even with all your research and interviews, you thought your brother was gay. That's exactly what we were trying to protect you from . . . people like you."

31

"Paloma, that bow is almost as large as my daughter's head. Are you sure about that? I don't know if I'll be able to keep the butterflies out of it."

She laughed so much that even he and Jazarah joined in. "She will be very chic. This is a gift from your sister, so I am certain she would never select anything to make your daughter look like a bumpkin."

Greg arrived at Nina's house, unbuckled Jazarah, lifted her out of her car seat, and onto the sidewalk. He smoothed her pink smocked sundress and adjusted her pink bow just slightly off-center as Paloma showed him. "Okay, hold daddy's hand and let's go meet Nina and Manny."

Hearing Manny bark, Jazarah pushed in a bit closer to Greg. Nina opened the door, and Greg realized he hadn't checked the affection protocol for child of single dad meeting . . . what was Nina? Surely not girlfriend and boyfriend. That might have worked ten years ago. Or longer. More than a friend, less than a fiancé? The complications were exhausting, which was why many single parents stayed home, popped popcorn, and rented DVDs. Just gave up dating until the kids hit high school or older.

Lately, though, with Nina in his life, Greg considered himself one of the fortunates. Since Nina continued to say yes, Greg assumed she enjoyed his company as well. He prayed she continued to want to be with him, but he trusted that God had a path. He just needed to keep putting one foot in front of the other.

For now, all he had to do was walk forward to Nina and feel the curve of her cheek in his hand as he kissed her on the forehead. His daughter, still held his hand, but leaned as far as she could without letting go to peek at Manny, resting in his crate.

Nina crouched down to eye-level with Jazarah, introduced herself as a friend of her daddy's, and offered her hand for a handshake. Which she promptly took and pulled Nina closer and hugged her neck. Greg felt as concerned as he did comforted. Though Greg told Paloma she had to stay until she was ninety, he knew the day would come when his daughter's nanny might want to have a life somewhere else with someone else. He tried not to think about it because the separation for all of them, but especially for Jazarah, would be brutal. Yet, his relationship with Nina, while he wanted it to be more, was still, what did Elise call it, marinating. "Sooner or later, you have to get cooking," she said.

When Greg and Jazarah moved closer, Manny thumped his tail, and stayed perfectly still while Jazarah's little hand wiggled through the sides to pet him. She smiled at her father. "I yike him," she announced.

"I yike him, too," said Nina.

"Thanks, Manny," Greg whispered as they started to leave. "Tell the puppy good-bye," he said to his daughter. She turned and smiled sweetly and waved at the dog. "Bye-Bye, Ne Na."

Nina smiled. "The kid's got my number already."

"Definitely not just a kid's place," Greg said, awed by the simulated tropical rainforest that was the Cockrell Butterfly Center. A fifty-foot waterfall fell from the top of the three-story glass building that housed a lush pathway lined with exotic plants and flowers from top to bottom. Butterflies were everywhere, hundreds of them . . . like finely

286

drawn artwork dripping with color flying around and through and over and under foliage and people and sprays from the waterfall.

Nina asked Jazarah if she could remove her bow. Greg waited to see if there would be a standoff. "Your bow is so beautiful, a butterfly might think it was a flower and not be able to get out. And that would be sad." Nina summoned a woeful expression as she spoke, and the performance paid off. Off came the bow, which she held as they walked along the path, and waved away a few curious butterflies.

Three floors of butterflies was Jazarah's limit, especially when one landing on her hand sent her into ambulance siren mode. When Greg suggested lunch, she applauded. He told Nina, "Guess that means it's time to eat."

They walked to a nearby deli for sandwiches, Jazarah between them, holding her hands and swinging her over cracks in the sidewalk. Greg appreciated how relaxed Nina was with his daughter. Sometimes people without children tended to get crazed about things that didn't matter. Things that, once you became a parent, you realized were insignificant. Like it wasn't important to wake a sleeping child to put

287

her jammies on. Sleeping in play clothes was not going to lower IQ points or permanently damage their self-esteem.

Jazarah invited Nina to help her color the maze on her placemat. Filling in the lines with her green crayon, Nina asked Greg questions about his relief work, and when he planned to start working full time at Dr. Maxwell's clinic. Greg answered, but Nina seemed distracted. Entirely too focused on staying inside the lines, and not focused enough on the conversation.

After his daughter lined up her chicken fingers with the "just right" squirt of catsup, Greg asked Nina if she wanted to join them next weekend at the Children's Museum.

Nina chewed, sipped her tea, cleared her throat, and fluffed her napkin. There weren't many other distractions available unless she aligned Jazarah's French Fries with her chicken strips.

Greg swirled a fry in his daughter's mountain of catsup and received a stern warning to not eat her food, "Mine," she warned him, shaking a fry in his direction. She eyed him for a few more bites, then rearranged her pickle slices.

"Nina, did you hear me, about the Children's Museum? Would you want to go? I thought we could ask Luke and Aretha to join us. For some reason, those places are just as much fun for adults who don't have legitimate play time anymore."

"I heard. I'm sorry," said Nina. "I'm not sure yet if I'll be able to do that . . ."

"No need to apologize. It's wrong of me to assume you might not have other plans," he said. Greg didn't consider that she might be seeing someone else. Someone whose idea of an event didn't include shopping in the make-believe grocery store and arguing over who ran the cash register.

She looked around like she'd dropped an answer on the floor somewhere. Clearly, she had something to tell him. "I didn't plan to talk about this here."

"Unless it's something unfit for my daughter's ears, it's going to be here. You can't look as if you just left a horror movie and expect me not to wonder what you saw there."

"Then please don't ask me any questions until I'm finished, okay?"

He nodded, and she began.

As Nina explained the offer she and Elise discussed, Greg felt like someone about to be pushed off a ledge. He couldn't stop it, and he had no idea if there would be anything to hold on to on the way down. He controlled his voice so as not to alarm his daughter, but he wasn't sure if he'd be able to maintain it for the entire conversation. "You're moving to New York? As in the next week or so? I . . . I had no idea that was even on the menu."

"Neither did I. I thought it was off the menu, then it came back on."

Now he colored with Jazarah, not bothering at all with lines and making ever animal purple. He listened to Nina detail the Janie, Brady, Daisy show that was now becoming a one-woman show, featuring his woman. Or at least the one he had hoped would be.

A herd of what looked like high school kids sat at the next table. Greg almost paid them to stay, so he didn't have to be the loudest voice in what was quite a small restaurant. "Is this position one you have to fill?"

She narrowed her eyes, and he knew that was a precursor to the defensive position, but he couldn't make himself stop. "So, you're absolutely choosing to go." The crayon tip snapped off as he spoke. After Jazarah's "Uh oh," he took the one she handed him. "Say what, Daddy?"

He'd forgotten the very manners he wanted her to learn. "Thank you, princess."

She smiled and continued giving all the people green faces. Greg wanted a distraction while Nina spoke, especially one that meant he didn't have to have eye contact. His animals became red.

"No one's forcing me. No one needs to. Managing editor of the New York office is something I've dreamed about for years. How could I pass up this opportunity?" She creased her napkin edges with her thumb as she spoke, so he knew he wasn't the only person feeling like a balloon about to explode. "Elise told me to take my time, but the reality is, I've been thinking about this for years. And don't ask me if I've prayed about it because I don't do prayer."

"Why?"

"Because Thomas died anyway. If praying isn't going to fix anything, what's the point?"

"I hafta potty," said Jazarah, who, between coloring, had arranged most of the food on her plate in straight lines without eating hardly any of it.

"Would you like to come with me?" Nina held out her hand.

"Peas," his daughter answered. "I be back, daddy." She flashed him a smile that pinched something in his chest that he knew must be reserved for daughters.

Greg called Paloma to ask her if she'd be able to keep J. a few hours. For better or for worse, this conversation with Nina had to happen tonight.

Nina was grateful Jazarah knew the words to Bob Marley's songs because she provided the entertainment on their way back to Greg's house. He'd already talked to her about dropping J. off and going somewhere else. She suggested the park near her house.

When they arrived at Greg's, Paloma walked outside to retrieve Jazarah. She and Greg discussed something about dinner and medicines, then he kissed his daughter good-bye. Nina had been checking her cell phone messages while they spoke, so the knock on the car window startled her.

"Kiss. Bye-Bye to Ne Na?"

"Of course," she said. *How did this kid wheedle her way in so quickly?*

Greg pulled out of the driveway and turned to Nina. "You see the problem already, don't you?"

She saw it, and she felt it. *Am I supposed to allow a three-year-old to determine my decisions? One who isn't even mine?* But she didn't know what to do about it. "I understand what you're saying, but I'm not sure what you want me to do. Jazarah is a precious child. How could I not adore her?"

"Exactly. You can adore her. But you can't

adore her then leave her. She's been through that already. And, fortunately for her, she's too young to remember her birth mother being the first woman to do that."

Nina talked to the window and the blurs of billboards and shops and offices that stretched between their homes. "Greg, I'm not doing this *to* you. I'm doing this for myself."

At the red light, he reached across the seat and covered her hand with his. "I get it, Nina, I really do. But, and maybe this is selfish on my part. I thought we were working toward something here between the two of us. The three of us."

She wished her hand didn't like the way his felt. It made this conversation all the more difficult. "Well, I thought so too . . ."

Greg let go to take the exit off the freeway. "Then why are you leaving? Could you consider, maybe, that all the things that have happened in your life and mine have brought us to this point for a reason? That your wanting to be a part of something important that can affect the world doesn't have to happen in New York? God is showering you with so many blessings, and you're running around looking for an umbrella."

"Well, it can rain in New York too, right?"

In the driveway, Greg shifted into park, but he didn't turn the engine off.

"I thought we were walking to the park," Nina said.

Greg leaned back against the headrest, closed his eyes for a moment, and turned to her. "Here's the thing. I care about you, I enjoy being with you, and I thought we could spend more time together . . . figure out where this might take us. But, if you decide that you want to stay there, I'm not moving to New York to start a veterinary practice to see if we can make things work. Elise, Peyton, Paloma, and Jazarah. My family is here."

"Maybe it won't work out, and I'll just be right back where I was before at *Trends*. And then we could . . ." She pushed the button to let the window down. Even the muggy air outside helped balance the sharpness of what she felt sitting next to Greg.

Greg shook his head. "We could, what? Jazarah and I could wait for you. Just in case you decided to come back? We're the consolation prize?"

"That's not what I meant at all."

"It's not my place to ask you to stay or to tell you to go. And since you didn't feel the need to discuss it with me before today, maybe that's something I need to think about. This is your decision. I wish it was yours and God's. I don't want my daughter in the next few weeks to grow attached to you. I don't want her to have to suffer through your leaving. And, what I'm about to say is so painful, I don't even want to hear myself say it. But, since you've made this decision, I think it's best we just stop where we are."

32

"Please don't make me tell him good-bye one more time." Nina closed her eyes and held up her hand so Aretha would stop handing Manny to her. "It's bad enough the two of you had to get him a car seat, and he took the ride to the airport with us."

The exhaust from the cars, the taxis, and buses burned Nina's nose. At least that's the excuse she gave Luke for why her face was red and puffy, from the constant sniffling. As Luke emptied the trunk of Nina's bags, Aretha went through the roll call of tickets, purse, keys, cell phone, cash. . . .

"Got it. Got it. Got it."

Aretha handed Manny to Luke and held out her arms. "I'm praying for you, even if you can't pray for yourself. I love you, and you need to be careful. Call as soon as your plane lands, okay?"

Nina hugged her and wished that when she let go, she could take some of Aretha with her. She kissed Manny, who tried to wiggle his way out of Luke's arms. She stood on her tiptoes, hugged Luke, and ordered him to take care of her friend. "She needs someone to watch her."

He smiled. "I know. That's my job, and I'm good at it."

"I can't do this. We have to go," said Aretha. She turned to Nina on her way back to the car, "You know, no decision has to be forever."

Nina nodded, afraid if she spoke it would be to tell them she changed her mind. Before Luke pulled away from the curb, Nina walked into the terminal. She couldn't bear to hear Manny's yelps or watch the car become smaller and smaller until it finally disappeared.

She detoured into the nearest bathroom, took a deep breath, checked for mascara runs, and lectured herself. *This is want you wanted, worked for, and dreamed about. This is your opportunity. You earned this.* The woman she saw in the mirror still didn't look convinced.

Nina found the gate for her flight. She checked in her baggage, went through security, and looked for a place to eat breakfast. When she finally sat, choosing a place with just a few customers, the past two weeks of her life filled every empty chair at the table and then some. Elise, everyone at the office, Daisy, Shannon, Luke, Aretha, . . .

The interview with Martha nearly wiped her out, but Elise told her it was her best one yet. Nina sent notes to all the Threads of Hope people thanking them for opening their lives to her so that others could have hope.

Aretha's quilt had been under her bed for so long, she'd almost forgotten about it. But she'd wrapped the box before she left, and Luke was going to give it to her today. Nina decided it would be her good-bye gift instead of her birthday one.

Every time her cell phone rang, she hoped the name Greg Hernandez would flash on the screen. But it didn't. The time she and Elise were together, neither one of them mentioned his name. A boundary neither one of them wanted to cross.

She'd had dinner on Thomas's birthday with her parents. They moved around the house as if they were strangers in an elevator, careful not to invade each other's personal space. Nina wished she'd bought a cake. They could have celebrated the years they all had with Thomas. After finding out about her brother, she just didn't know how they could mend all that had broken for them as a family. Maybe, being away would help with that. Give her perspective.

Nina shivered, and rubbed her arms with her hands. What possessed her to wear a sleeveless dress on the plane? The person next to her would probably set the air on Arctic chill. Aretha thought the deep kiwi cotton dress was classic and made a statement. Nina hoped she remembered to tell her that whatever statement Aretha thought she heard, it was all wrong.

The waitress brought her a menu and poured her a cup of coffee. "Here you go. That should warm you up," she said and made the last three words sound like one, warmyaup. A snapshot of Jazarah reminding Greg to say "thank you" flashed before her. She blinked, and it was gone. She thanked the waitress who said that she'd be back for her order. "No rush," she said.

Nina set her cell phone on the table hanging on a thread of hope that Greg would call. Or like Richard Gere in *An Officer and a Gentleman,* he'd whip through the airport in his white lab jacket, scoop her up like she's Debra Winger, and carry her out of the terminal. *Why? So you could blame him if the staying behind didn't work out?* Nina closed her eyes until the silly romantic image disappeared. She didn't need Greg to save her from herself.

She propped her legs on the chair across from her while she scanned the menu. The Belgian waffles with whipped cream and pecans were winning out over the Blueberry Blintzes, but the omelets held promise.

Nina felt a tap on her shoulder and, though an odd way of taking an order, she thought it was the waitress. "Oh, I haven't decided what I want yet . . ."

"We could tell," the man standing behind her said.

"Can I help you?" Nina said to the couple, who appeared to be in their seventies, as they made their way around the table. She made sure her purse was zipped and still on the chair next to her.

The woman wore an ash gray peplum jacket and a gored skirt that matched. *Definitely not a flight attendant.* The man next to her was dressed in a charcoal-shaded suit that had a faint gray pinstripe, and his silver tie was almost the same shade as his hair. "Actually," the woman said, her eyes almost as dark as Nina's coffee, "we were going to ask if we could help you. Weren't we, Daniel?"

Nina looked around for cameras. Maybe this was some weird reality television show.

There were still a dozen or so empty tables in the restaurant, so this wasn't the last place to sit.

He nodded. "That's right. We just thought you looked like you could use some company and, well, it's just Roberta and me traveling by ourselves, too."

Nina moved her legs off the chair, already a bit depressed her solitariness was a lighthouse beacon over her head. Greg's yammering on about trust wound its way through her brain. Her conscience shrugged its shoulders and said, *Might as well do a test run here, Nina. You're about to start the great adventure of your life.* Nina pulled out a chair, "Sure, have a seat. My name's Nina. And you are Roberta and . . . ?"

"Happy to meet you, Nina. My name is Daniel," he said and stood behind his chair until Roberta was comfortably seated in her own before he sat next to her.

The man seemed almost senatorial, and Nina's reporter brain whirred into action. She didn't want to see a newspaper later to discover she'd had no clue that she shared a breakfast table with a distinguished politician and his bride. But none of the files her brain flipped through made any connection. Still, they seemed to have that patina of gentility that grew more beautiful with age, and she hoped her brain hadn't misplaced an important file.

The waitress walked over. "Well, look at you. Made friends already," she said and pulled her pen out her apron pocket. "Y'all know what you want?"

That's why I'm here. Alone. Having breakfast with two elderly strangers. Nina searched the menu one more time. "I'll have the waffles. No, make that the blintzes." She handed the menu over and regretted she didn't stick with the waffles. Roberta and Daniel ordered coffee.

"Sharing those blintzes?" The waitress, eyes narrowed, looked at the couple.

Daniel smiled. "Actually, we've already eaten breakfast."

"Okey-dokey. Whatever," she said as if she'd been defeated.

Why are they stalking breakfast cafes if they've already eaten? Nina thought her conscience might be too eager for new experiences. She'd have to be careful to not disclose too much information about herself.

Roberta asked where Nina was headed. "New York. New job. I'll be working as an editor for a magazine." So much for careful.

They both nodded. "That sounds quite exciting," said Roberta.

Nina almost told her why she was so excited. She ushered her enthusiasm away, and asked, "And you? Where are you two going?"

They looked at one another and turned the same shade of blush pink. "You're probably going to laugh, but we'll tell you anyway. Partly why we wanted some company. Nobody to share our good news with."

Nina's journalist ears perked up. "Good news? I could use some. Spill it."

Roberta leaned toward Nina and whispered, "We're going on our honeymoon." Daniel nodded and smiled. He couldn't seem to stop doing either one.

"Honeymoon? Really?" Nina sipped her coffee, grateful she didn't laugh as they'd expected. How could she when their faces glowed like soft lamp light?

The waitress returned with two cups of coffee and Nina's breakfast. "There ya go, honey. Belgium waffles with whipped cream and pecans."

"But I ordered the blintzes," said Nina. *Didn't I?*

She reached for Nina's plate. "I can take these back. Thought for sure you said waffles."

"No problem. These are great," Nina told her. "Really."

She mumbled as she walked away.

Nina separated the waffles and spread the whipped cream over each. "Oh, so you renewed your wedding vows?"

"No. We just made them," said Daniel. He reached out and put his arm around his bride. "Just this morning we did." Roberta rested her head on his shoulder when he hugged her, then gently patted his chest. "Now Daniel, we shouldn't make a scene in public." When he let go, Nina didn't miss the fact that he moved his hand so that it rested on her knee.

"So, you just got married this morning, and you're leaving to go where on your honeymoon?"

"We're going to Hawaii," Daniel said. "We think it's time we learned how to surf. Don't you?"

Nina hesitated. If Roberta laughed, so would she. But she didn't. "We registered for private lessons. At our age, we didn't want the young people in a group to worry about us having heart attacks the first time we tried to stand on our boards."

Aretha would love this couple. Nina was quite infatuated with them already. Nina's stomach wasn't so infatuated with butter and whipped cream as breakfast choices and grumbled its disapproval. She set her fork on her plate and checked her cell phone. *Just in case.* Still silent. And so were Roberta and Daniel. Nina looked up from her phone. "I'm sorry. That was rude of me."

"We all get distracted, especially when we're not sure what we're looking for," said Daniel. He clasped Roberta's hand, intertwining their fingers so that their polished wedding bands, his next to hers, seemed to connect one to the other. "For a long time, we both had . . .' he looked at his wife. "What's that called?"

"Shiny ball syndrome." She leaned toward Nina and whispered, "His grandson told us about that."

"Guess I forget it because I don't want to remember having it. We spent too many years of our lives chasing after jobs that glittered, shiny things, even people we thought sparkled. Everything loses its shine after a while. It's what we're left with after the newness wears off that matters."

Roberta laughed. "I think we're proof God has a sense of humor, you know? But we learned the hard way that when our time is over here, no person in his right mind says, 'Wish I would have spent one more day at the office.' "

Daniel and Roberta left for their flight to Maui, and Nina gathered herself for the walk to her gate. She thought about what they'd said . . . about no one ever regretting the time they spent with the people they love. Did being alone in the job she dreamed of trump being with those she cared about, in the job that allowed her to be there with them?

Nina thought about her life, the one she was leaving behind. How many times the unexpected had provided for her, how the very boy she detested in high school grew to be the man who made her a better person, how being given the opportunity to attend the benefit resulted in the feature stories that could change lives.

And who made all that happen, Nina? Who brought that together, stitch by stitch, threading pieces of lives together to create something extraordinary? Just because you don't see Me, that doesn't mean I'm not there. Would you want Thomas to have lived longer if it meant being in pain? Was that prayer for you or for him?

Your entire life, you wanted to belong, to be loved, to be a part of something that could make a difference . . . and you had it. Just where you were.

Those were the desires of your heart, Nina. New York is the desire of your ego.

What if she gave God another chance? What if she prayed for Greg to meet her at the airport? That would prove God heard her, how could she not have faith after that?

Nina waited until she heard the final call before she handed over her boarding pass. Another prayer unanswered. Another loss. Another reason to doubt.

33

"Elise, this is the third consecutive year you've called the night of the benefit to ask about picking me up," Greg said as he checked his tuxedo pockets for his cuff links.

He heard Peyton through the speakerphone. "That's because she's stubborn. I told her —"

"Please don't shout. You'll upset the baby."

Greg laughed. "The baby isn't due for another two months."

"Babies hear sounds eighteen weeks into a pregnancy, and loud noises startle them. I've done my research. I don't want her traumatized before she's born," Elise said.

"She? When did you find that out?" He checked his pants pockets. Still no cufflinks.

"We didn't. I just alternate between using her and him. We still want to be surprised."

"Whatever makes you happy. In the meantime, I don't want one of your surprises to be us being there late. I'm looking for my cufflinks, and she's almost ready." The bedroom door opened, and Greg smiled. "In fact, she's ready now. We'll be there soon."

Jazarah pranced in and stood in front of the full-length mirror and twirled. Her sapphire dress sparkled almost as brightly as her eyes. "You are so pretty," she said to her reflection. "Right, Daddy?"

Greg lifted her, kissed her forehead, and whirled her around. "You are beautiful, my little princess." As her feet touched the floor, he noticed they were still bare. "You can't go to the ball without shoes."

Paloma entered after a faint knock at the bedroom door. "She escaped to your room before her shoes and her sash. A few more minutes, and she will be dressed." She held her hand out to Jazarah, "Come, princess. It's almost time for you to leave, but you need to finish getting dressed."

His daughter blew him a kiss, and she skipped out of his room, her dark curls bouncing.

Again the door opened. "I found a pair of lovely silver monogrammed cufflinks. They must be yours since you're the only man in the house who'd be wearing them."

"You are not only beautiful, but useful in emergencies," Greg said before he kissed

Nina. "This never gets old," he whispered and kissed her again.

"We have to stop now or we'll never make it to the benefit," she whispered back, her voice warm and silky. "I promise we'll pick up where we left off when we return."

"I'm a lucky man," Greg said and held out his arms so Nina could put his cufflinks on.

"Lucky? No. Smart? Yes." Her eyes drank in this man whose wife she had become because he trusted God. And, in doing so, showed her how to trust Him as well. Almost two years ago, she'd stepped out of a plane determined to start the life she'd dreamed of for years. When God didn't answer her prayer for Greg to meet her at the airport in Houston, by the time she arrived at JFK, she'd decided she could live without both of them.

Nina was on the phone with Aretha waiting for her baggage when someone tapped her on the shoulder. *What is it today with this shoulder tapping?* She turned around and found herself face-to-face with Greg.

He took the cell phone from her. "Hi, Aretha. She'll call you back." He ended the call and handed her the phone. "Do you need help with your suitcases?"

"Help with my suitcases? Are you kidding

me?" She swatted her bangs off her forehead and resisted the urge to bash him over his head with her purse. "What are you doing here, and how did you know I was talking to Aretha?"

"Is this your way of telling me you're happy to see me?" He reached for her hand. "Let's talk over here. Away from the crowd."

Nina remembered looking around the airport to convince herself she hadn't fallen through some worm hole and into another life. She recognized the faces of passengers who were on the same flight, and she spotted her luggage as the conveyor burped it out of the belly of the plane. So she had landed exactly where she'd intended. But she was no less confused than she was before. "Look, I don't know how or why you're here. All your talk about faith and trust and prayer I prayed and waited and waited and waited for you to meet me at the airport —"

His hands cradled her face. "Well here I am. At the airport."

And that was her first lesson in understanding that answered prayer may look different than she expected.

And she could not have expected, standing in the airport baggage claim that day, the blessings that awaited her in the life she and Greg shared today.

He straightened his bow tie and turned to Nina, "Well? Should I whirl around like our daughter so you can see how beautiful I am?"

She laughed. "I should have made you sign a 'non-compete clause.' It's not fair that you turn more heads walking into a room than I do."

He sighed. "It's a curse I live with daily," he said but couldn't maintain his serious expression. Greg tapped his watch. "You have less than ten minutes to be stunning and ready to roll. And you're still waltzing around in your robe."

"Go check on Jazarah. Oh, and please make sure she's not trying to feed Manny. Or that he's not curled up in her lap or —"

"Should I be taking notes?" He looked at her with that lop-sided smile she knew characterized his sarcasm.

"No, dear. I'm the freelance writer in the family, remember? All I have to do is slip on my dress."

He sat on the edge of their bed. "Then maybe I'll wait . . ."

"Get out of here or else you'll suffer the wrath of hormonal Elise when we arrive late." She kissed his forehead. As he walked out, she said, "And, anyway, I know you won't leave without me."

He'd told her that when he'd surprised her at the airport. Greg said that Elise and his memories provided the fuel he needed to go after his own dream. His sister had called him and asked him why he was still home. "You may not like what Nina is doing, but she's at least going after what she thinks she wants. That takes courage. You, on the other hand . . ." He ended the conversation without letting her finish. Pacing in the den, he passed photographs of his parents and of Lily. Three people he loved, taken from him, by people and situations over which he had no control. *Will you let Nina be number four? Can you live the rest of your life knowing you never let her know you loved her?* He called Elise to apologize. "Accepted," she said. "Now, get to the airport because I already booked your flight out."

Over vending machine canned drinks and cheese crackers near baggage claim, Greg placed two tickets on the table. "I won't leave without you. Unless you want me to. If New York is what you want, then I'll tear one up and be on my way. But I couldn't let you go without telling you that what I want is a life with you."

Her second lesson in understanding: sometimes the answer appeared before the question. New York wasn't just an answer to a dream, it was the stuffing that filled the void of recognition, importance, self-worth. *And then what?* She pictured Daniel's and Roberta's faces, their joy so transparent she could see their hearts. Was she afraid to be that happy?

Her fingertips grazed the ticket. She couldn't bring herself to look at Greg. "I don't deserve this. Or you. I don't even know why God would do something for me. I've ignored Him almost my entire life."

He placed his hand under her chin and lifted her face to his. "None of us deserve happiness. That's what makes it a gift. And loving us even when we've ignored Him? That's why He's God, and we're not."

Elise's pregnancy was not only a happy surprise for her, but also one for Nina who would be wearing the dress Elise had ordered for herself. A one-shouldered sheer black tulle, the dress was offset at the waist by an Art Deco enamel pin set with glass pearls and Swarovski crystal. She'd just slipped it on when Paloma's voice came from the other side of the closet door. "Sorry to disturb you, but someone wanted to see you."

Nina stepped out and, as always, experienced the exquisite joy of seeing their son. His arms and legs churned the air as Paloma handed him to her. Thomas greeted her with a chorus of "ma-ma-ma-ma" with intermittent sprays from the motorboat imitation he learned from his big sister.

Careful to avoid the pin on her dress, Nina transferred him to her hip and covered his face with kisses. He rewarded her with throaty giggles and a few more sprays, kicking his legs against her as if in a horse race. "One of these days, I suppose you'll have hair," she said as she caressed the blonde stubble on his head. Thomas's eyes darted back and forth across Nina's face. His mouth made a tiny "o" as he reached out a plump little hand and grabbed one of her diamond earrings.

While Nina balanced him, Paloma carefully unwound his chubby fingers from around the loops Nina wore. "He's definitely his father's son. When he sees what he wants, he goes for it," said Nina. "Be sweet tonight." She kissed him on each cheek, then turned him over to Paloma.

"Let's read a story, Mr. Thomas," she said. They left the room, her son babbling as if every syllable told a story.

Nina learned another important lesson through their son. Though the death of her

315

brother Thomas devastated the O'Malley family, the birth of her son brought a promise of healing. Her relationship with her parents was still fragile, but their grandson awakened a hope in them that had been long ago buried. She and Greg gave them tickets for the We Care benefit tonight, and they said they would attend. Aretha and Luke were picking them up to make sure because Nina did not want her parents to miss the surprise she'd planned. Threads of Hope quilted a panel in honor of Thomas, and they would be taking it with them to Washington next week.

"Nina? We're walking to the car . . ."

That was her husband's two-minute warning. Nina made one last check in the mirror. She ran her fingers through her still short layers of curls to fluff what Thomas had flattened, made sure she didn't have lipstick on her teeth, and covered herself with one final spritz of perfume. She was about to walk away when she heard a familiar voice.

You're beautiful, Nina. You always were.

She whispered, "Thank you" and went downstairs to meet Greg, Jazarah, and the future they were stitching together.

DISCUSSION QUESTIONS
(SPOILER ALERT!)

1. When we first meet Nina, her single focus is the New York promotion. Is her self-worth connected to her job? Why? Do you find that, today, many people are like Nina in that they are defined by the work/career/profession they have chosen? If so, why? If not, why not?

2. What is Nina's relationship with her parents, especially her mother? Is Nina judging her harshly, is Sheila a harsh judge, or both? What is it that mothers and daughters expect and want from one another? How is that different for sons, or is it?

3. For more than ten years, Nina carries the high school incident with Greg Hernandez and his friends. What happened to this grudge over time? Did it shape the woman she became? Why is Nina holding on to those negative feelings?

4. What does Nina see in Aretha and Daisy

that led her to consider them friends? Why doesn't either one of them or both discuss the New York decision with her? Should they have? At what point are we willing to risk the relationship with friends by honestly sharing about situations in their lives?

5. What, if any, of the information about The AIDS Memorial Quilt is new to you? Does its size surprise you? If you were already in a city where some of the panels were being displayed, would you go to the exhibit? Why or why not?

6. Were you already aware of the number of children who die in Third World countries because of AIDS? Would you have adopted Jazarah? Why or why not? Does it concern you that children like her are being assimilated into our schools and society at large?

7. The stories the families shared were all different. Were they what you expected?

8. Should Nina's parents have told her the truth about Thomas? Were their reasons for not telling her justifiable? What would you have done in the same situation, same time? Would bringing this forward to the twenty-first century make a difference in Nina's parents' decision? In yours?

9. Do you agree with Nina's decision not to stay in New York?

10. Greg ends their relationship when Nina tells him about going to New York. Do you think he is being unnecessarily overprotective of his daughter and her feelings?

INSTRUCTIONS FOR MAKING A QUILT PANEL

THE NAMES
PROJECT FOUNDATION:
THE AIDS MEMORIAL QUILT
Step by Step: How to Make a Panel For The Quilt

You don't have to be an artist or sewing expert to create a moving personal tribute remembering a life lost to AIDS, but you do have to make a panel in order to add a name to The Quilt. It's not as complicated as many people think, though. It doesn't matter if you use paint or fine needlework, iron-on transfers or handmade appliqués, or even spray paint on a sheet; any remembrance is appropriate. (This is, however, the only way to have a name added to The Quilt — by making a panel to remember your lost loved one.) You may choose to create a panel privately as a personal memorial or you may choose to follow the traditions of old-fashioned quilting bees by including friends, family, and co-workers. That choice, like virtually everything else involved in making a panel, is completely up to you.

Here, in a few easy steps, is how to create a panel for The Quilt:

1. Design the panel

Include the name of the person you are remembering. Feel free to include additional information such as the dates of birth and death, hometown, special talents, etc. We ask that you please limit each panel to one individual (obvious exceptions include siblings or spouses).

2. Choose your materials

Remember that The Quilt is folded and unfolded every time it is displayed, so durability is crucial. Since glue deteriorates with time, it is best to sew things to the panel. A medium-weight, non-stretch fabric such as a cotton duck or poplin works best.

Your design can be vertical or horizontal, but the finished, hemmed panel must be 3 feet by 6 feet (90 cm × 180 cm) — no more and no less! When you cut the fabric, leave an extra 2-3 inches on each side for a hem. If you can't hem it yourself, we'll do it for you. Batting for the panels is not necessary, but backing is recommended. Backing helps to keep panels clean when they are laid out on the ground. It also helps retain the shape of the fabric.

3. Create the panel

In constructing your panel, you might want to use some of the following techniques:

- Appliqué: Sew fabric, letters, and small mementos onto the background fabric. Do not rely on glue — it won't last.

- Paint: Brush on textile paint or color-fast dye, or use an indelible ink pen. Please don't use "puffy" paint; it's too sticky.

- Stencils: Trace your design onto the fabric with a pencil, lift the stencil, then use a brush to apply textile paint or use indelible markers.

- Collage: Make sure that whatever materials you add to the panel won't tear the fabric (avoid glass and sequins for this reason), and be sure to avoid very bulky objects.

- **Photos:** The best way to include photos or letters is to photocopy them onto iron-on transfers, iron them onto 100% cotton fabric and sew that fabric to the panel. You may also put the photo in clear plastic vinyl and sew it to the panel (off-center so it avoids the fold).

4. Write a letter

Please take the time to write a letter about the person you've remembered. The letter might include your relationship to him or her, how he or she would like to be remembered, and a favorite memory. If possible, please send us a photograph along with the letter for our archives.

5. Make a donation

If you are able, please make a donation to help pay for the cost of adding your panel to The Quilt. The NAMES Project Foundation depends on the support of panel makers to preserve the Quilt and keep it on display. Gifts of any amount are welcome and greatly appreciated.

6. Fill out the panel maker information form

This provides us with vital information about you and your panel.

7. Send in the panel

Once your panel is completed there are several ways you can submit it to The NAMES Project so that it becomes a part of The AIDS Memorial Quilt.

You can send your panel to The NAMES Project Foundation or you can opt to bring the panel to a Quilt display or to a local chapter.

Send it to us directly at The NAMES Project Foundation

ATTN: New Panels
The NAMES Project Foundation
204 14TH ST NW
ATLANTA, GA 30318-5304
404.688.5500

Be sure to send it by registered mail or with a carrier that will track your package. We recommend panels be shipped via Federal Express or UPS.

Bring the panel to a Quilt display

Please be sure to contact the local display host first for more information on how and when they are collecting new panels (many displays accept new panels only on the last day of the event, while others are prepared to accept new panels at any time during a display).

Bring a new panel to one of our chapters
Your panel will stay in the community for up to three months, being used for education and outreach, and then will be sent to the Foundation to be sewn into the Quilt.

Important
No matter how you decide to turn in a new panel, please be sure to print out the panel maker information form, fill it out, and include it with the panel. This information helps us to stay in touch with you and keep you up to date on both the panel and The Quilt.

How your panel becomes part of The Quilt
When a new panel arrives at our national headquarters in Atlanta, it is carefully logged and examined for durability. Some panels might require hemming to adjust for size; others may need reinforcement or minor repairs. Next, new panels are sorted — some grouped geographically by region, others by theme or appearance. When eight similar panels are collected, they are sewn together to form a twelve-foot square. This is the basic building block of The Quilt, and

it is usually referred to as either a "12-by-12" or "Block."

Once sewn, each 12-by-12 is edged in canvas and given a unique number, its "Block Number," which makes tracking the block possible. All panel, panel maker, and numerical information is then stored in our Quilt databases. Once this happens, you are sent information including which block the panel you submitted has been made a part of, how to request the block for displays of The Quilt, and a current display schedule.

The entire process, from our receiving the panel to incorporating it into a 12-by-12 in The AIDS Memorial Quilt, typically takes between three and six months.

Questions?

"The only dumb question is the question you have but never ask!" Email questions to: panels@aidsquilt.org or call Roddy Williams, Panel Maker Relations, or Gert McMullin, Production Manager, at 404.688.5500.

For information on panel making workshops contact: Jada Harris at 404-688-5500 ext. 228 or email jharris@aidsquilt.org.

Panel-Maker Partner
Buddy System

The NAMES Project Foundation is launching a new Panel-maker Partner buddy system that will pair volunteers with individuals wanting to make a panel for the Quilt. Creating a panel on your own might seem daunting but with the help of a partner the process is suddenly much more manageable. This is a way you can ensure that a friend or loved one lives on as part of this epic handmade memorial — the largest piece of community folk art in the world and one of our most powerful HIV prevention education tools. If you are interested, a member of The NAMES Project Staff will contact you for further information and to find out how you would like to share the process. (See www.aidsquilt.org/callmyname for a link to the form.)

Call My Name Project

Call My Name is a program designed to draw attention to a public health crisis by fostering the creation of new panels for The AIDS Memorial Quilt made by African Americans in honor of their friends, family, and community members who have died of AIDS. With the introduction of The AIDS Memorial Quilt, The NAMES Project redefined the tradition of quilt making in response to contemporary circumstances. Call My Name uses this model and through hands-on, panel-making activity brings people and communities together to remember loved ones, grieve, find support and strength, and engage in dialogues for change. Call My Name also enhances The NAMES Project's ability to collect and display greater numbers of panels that reflect the epidemic's impact within the African American community. As a result, Quilt prevention, education and awareness programs have greater capacity to deliver even more cultural relevance and provide poignant personal connections for African American men, women, and children who see it. (See http://www.aidsquilt.org/callmy name.)